THE DARK STAR

THE DARK STAR

H. R. Hess

Reformation
Lightning

Reformation Lightning

www.ReformationLightning.com

First published by Reformation Lightning in 2022

Cover design by JT Branding (www.jtbranding.com)

Printed and bound in Great Britain by Clays Ltd, Elcograf S.p.A.

ISBN 978-1-8381883-6-8

3 5 7 10 8 6 4 2

For Steffan,
who has supported me in everything,
from patiently listening to me rambling about
typesetting, maps, and dragons,
to giving me whole precious days to write.
I am so glad The Dark Star is
"better than you expected."

KEY

1 .... Sarreia

2 .... Lorandia

3 .... Faradel

4 .... Afrada

5 .... Lelanta

6 .... Hirath's Rift

7 .... Ubereth

8 .... Runa's shipwreck

9 .... Orr

10 ...... The battle line

MAP OF CALLENLAS

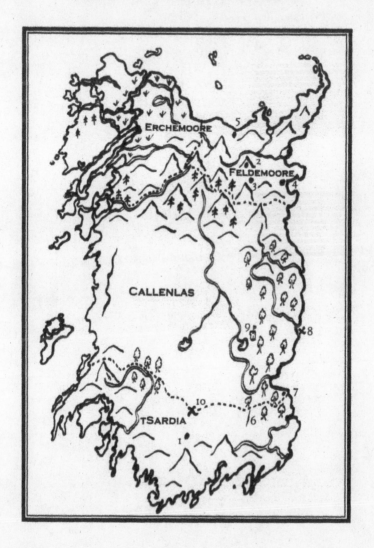

CHAPTER 1

Zaphreth stood alone under the stars, their light caught in his hair like dust. Under his feet, the desert sand still held the day's heat, and a warm southern wind eddied the surface like water.

Behind Zaphreth lay the city of Sarreia, the air heavy with the sighs of sleeping people and animals. Before him lay the desert, mile upon mile of ochre sand speckled with tufts of wiry, black grass, and spiky shrubs that offered no sustenance to man or beast. Beyond that lay the northern lands, and the border with Callenlas, Zaphreth's destination.

They had stories there, in Callenlas, that the stars had taken on human form. Father always ridiculed them.

"Children's fables," he said. "A load of old nonsense."

Zaphreth had believed him. Now, though, with a fearful mission awaiting him, his childhood happiness

1

in dust around his feet, Zaphreth's throat ached at the thought that someone might be able to see him, someone powerful and wise, and that they might even care about him. He raised his eyes to the stars winking in their bed of velvet.

Sarreia was almost entirely dark now, only a few lamps left shining bravely against the night. The night sky arced overhead in impossible vastness, the stars vivid and clear. Zaphreth could see hints of violet, amber and blue in their distant light. The beauty overhead was stunning, and for a moment he forgot his misery and apprehension, and the dangerous journey ahead of him.

He was fourteen, small for his age but with a wiry strength, and a shock of dark hair hanging into his eyes. To anyone looking on, he appeared to be just another blacksmith's apprentice, his tunic smudged from hours bent over a forge. But his eyes were a bright and startling blue, had anyone bothered to take a second look into a poor apprentice's face.

"Would you help me?" he murmured into the night, careful to keep the sound small, so the night watchmen on the walls would not hear him. "Would you help me if I asked you?"

The stars flickered remotely, unconcerned at his plight, and Zaphreth felt suddenly foolish.

"Children's stories," he muttered to himself bitterly. The

stars were just lights. No one knew where he was. No one cared. He was alone in the universe with no one to rely on but himself.

Lowering his head back to the dust, he shifted the pack on his back and scoured the bushes in frustration, trying to shake off his sense of desolation. Where was his guide? He had been assured that someone would meet him here to lead him to the northern border, and to one of the few places where he could cross safely into Callenlas. There was no moon, so it was harder to judge the passing of time, but half of the sea serpent constellation had dipped below the western horizon while he waited. Zaphreth pressed his lips together and wondered about using Mind Powers to light his palm and search the bushes, or to signal to the guide. In this vast expanse of darkness, it would be so easy to miss each other. But any light would alert the watchmen to his presence, and the mission was supposed to be top secret.

For a moment, the thought that the guide might not turn up and the whole thing might be called off made his heart clench with hope. Zaphreth was afraid of venturing over the border into enemy territory. The terror of what King Elior would do to him if he was caught lurked in the corners of his mind.

Zaphreth refused to look at it. If he let himself notice the fear fully, he would never find the courage to go. He squashed the hope firmly. If the guide did not show, he would find a way himself. Lord Lur did not accept failure.

"This is ridiculous," he muttered to himself. He would have to set out alone and hope the guide would be able to catch him up and find him on the road.

Zaphreth eased himself up, ready to walk eastward, when something glittered in the bush ten paces to his right. Zaphreth froze. Was it a guard? An animal?

He took a slow, nervous step out of his own clump of grass. The other bush moved too, though there was no breeze. Then out stepped a small, stocky figure, barely a hand's breadth taller than Zaphreth himself.

Zaphreth opened his mouth to greet the stranger, but the hooded head shook slowly, *no*. A dark hand gestured for Zaphreth to be silent, then beckoned, and began striding north-east towards the road.

The stranger moved swiftly and silently, apparently able to glide over the sand (which Zaphreth floundered gracelessly over), and to see in the dark (which Zaphreth stumbled repeatedly in). Once on the hard surface of the road, the stranger walked even faster, and Zaphreth was hard-pressed even to talk, had his companion permitted conversation.

Only once they were well away from the dark walls of Sarreia did the stranger pull back his hood a little and fix a pair of black, beady eyes on Zaphreth.

4

"Wirrat," he said, extending his hand to Zaphreth for their palms to meet in the gesture of peace.

"Zaphreth," he replied, with a gulp of air, for the pace continued as brisk as ever.

"You're small," the man said, narrowing those eyes to scan Zaphreth up and down, taking in his wiry body, the ill-fitting tunic, and the shaggy black hair that hung into his blue eyes. "Young."

"Lord Lur chose me," Zaphreth asserted, holding out his hand near Wirrat's face so that he could see the thin, pale scar that crossed his palm.

Wirrat raised his eyebrows but nodded, turning back to watch the road.

"We'll head east on the road for a few days, then turn north-east until we reach Hirath's Rift. The desert gives way to farmland there and the people are less bothered by war, less watchful. We should be able to slip over the border quite easily."

Zaphreth nodded. He wondered how a man with such short legs could keep up such a pace without losing his breath. Hoisting his pack higher, Zaphreth gritted his teeth and walked on over the desert.

CHAPTER 2

By craning her neck, Runa could see all the way down from the library window into the dragon enclosure. A bright green valley dragon was being separated from her year-old baby so that it could be trained. Her pointed tail flicked, a sure sign of anxiety, and her head was raised on her long throat. Runa could imagine the conflict of emotions coursing through the dragon, muscles flinching between her desire to obey her rider and her desire to protect her baby.

It seemed cruel, but the dragon's training had to begin young so that it could build a close relationship with its rider. If it was left any longer, the baby would be beyond taming. In the wild it would already be beginning to learn how to hunt, pulling away from the mother naturally.

"Princess Runa?" Master Greigon, Runa's tutor, had his lips pressed together tightly, and was rapping on his desk with his ruler. Runa jumped guiltily and tried to look as though she had been concentrating.

"The second largest river of Feldemoore?"

Runa glanced down at her paper where she had begun writing the answers to her test on her country's geography. So far, she had scrawled 'Peison', 'Taralai', and a few illegible letters which might have been the beginning of Lorandia but because she could not remember the question, she could not be sure. How many questions had she missed?

Master Greigon was pacing towards her from his desk, looking over her shoulder at the paper. The Day-Star's light poured in through the tall windows of Lorandia's library, falling on the stacks of scrolls lying on their shelves, as high as the ceiling. The carpets and exposed boards in between lay in rectangles of light and shade. The fine day made Runa itch to feel the light of the Day-Star on her arms and the wind in her hair.

Runa snatched at the moment to glance down into the dragon enclosure once again. The mother had been coaxed out by her rider, and now the gate was down, the baby was alone, his pale wings flapping with anxiety. Runa could see his selected rider, the newly elected Erandel, inching towards him with a piece of meat in his extended hand. Men had lost hands and arms trying to approach a newly weaned infant. Runa strained her neck ...

Snap! Master Greigon drew the blind down, blocking Runa's view.

Runa sank back into her chair, disappointed.

It was not fair, she thought to herself. Her brothers had had each other to make lessons interesting. They had studied interesting subjects like history, battle tactics and Elior's law. Runa was stuck with letter writing, basic geography and music. She also had dancing twice a week, which she was terrible at, and etiquette, which was even worse.

Runa's first love was dragons. As soon as she could hold a crayon, she had scrawled dragons on paper in her nursery, watching them circle the turrets of the castle from the window. Aged three she had escaped her nurses and scurried all the way down to the dragon caves. She was found hours later, still transfixed by the beautiful animals, when the castle was in uproar as night was falling and the princess was still missing. Oblivious to the chaos she had caused, Runa had lain awake long into the night, dreaming of the day she would be old enough to ride a dragon of her very own.

"Princess Runa." Master Greigon's patience was wearing thin. "I have been charged with your education and betterment. You do me a great disservice with your inattention. Worse, you dishonour your father and your people by your unwillingness to learn ..."

Runa sighed inwardly and began to dream of what it would be like to ride her dragon. Her favourite had changed over the years. As a small child she had always imagined riding the rare but vivid red fire dragons, the ones that spouted flames and whose scales were as bright as the setting Day-Star. Then she had admired the large blacks, with their steely scales and gleaming spines. Lately, she favoured the blue mountain dragons, their scales hued like clouds before rain, winding through the air like spirals of smoke. They were smaller, but quicker and lither than the larger variations of their species.

"I give up," Master Greigon sighed, before walking out of the library, leaving the door swinging on its hinges.

Runa's mouth twisted to one side as she considered the guilt that tugged at her insides. She never intended to be rude, or to ignore her tutors, but they managed to make the lessons so dull, and dragons were so very interesting. If they would only set her essays on the habits of dragons, or the history of their taming, or their care and uses in war. But all they wanted was for her to write boring invitations to imaginary courtiers, or remember the correct ways to address a Master, a princess and an ambassador. Hardly stuff to thrill her soul.

Leaving her desk, Runa checked the Day-Star's position outside the window. Master Greigon had left her half-way through the lesson; she would have time to run down to the dragon enclosure before her dancing lesson.

She left the library in haste, thumped down the stairs and continued through the palace to the kitchens, picking up a green apple from a basket on her way.

"Oi!" the cook scolded. But then she chuckled and sent the spit boy after Runa with a piece of fresh gingerbread, oozing stickiness. Runa grinned and ate it on her way through the kitchen gardens, licking her lips and fingers.

She stepped through the arched gateway that led to the dragon enclosure.

"Ow!" she cried as her ear was caught between a pinching finger and thumb.

"Just where do you think you are going?" Master Greigon demanded, his face purple with rage.

"I was just ..."

"Do you have so little regard for my word that you trip off to see the dragons as soon as I leave?"

"I ..." Runa writhed against the pain in her ear.

"I have reached the end! Come with me!"

Runa had little choice. He let go of her ear but caught her wrist in the same movement, dragging her back into the palace and up, up to King Mabrigas's rooms.

Runa's stomach tightened.

"No, please," she begged. "I'll study, I'll work hard ... please don't tell Father."

"Too late!" Greigon snapped, before storming past the page, who was waving his thin arms pathetically. Greigon pushed the king's door open so hard that it slammed into the shelves behind it and sent a stack of papers flying about the room from the desk, like leaves in a gust of wind.

"My King," Greigon bowed perfunctorily, and thrust Runa in front of him. "I give up! I cannot teach this girl anymore. She is beyond remedy!"

Runa stared aghast around her father's study. It was one of his smaller rooms, usually kept private for his own use, the walls lined with his favourite scrolls and leather-bound annals of the history of Feldemoore. His imposing desk stood by the window, looking out over the castle and small town of Lorandia to the lower mountains, and beyond to where the eastern sea glittered on the horizon. A fire crackled cosily in the large marble grate, but what made Runa stagger to a halt and gulp was not her father seated near the warming flames, but the figure of the ambassador for Taranata in the armchair opposite, his peculiar, pointed hat slightly askew. King Mabrigas never invited guests into his study. This must be a deeply private and highly important discussion.

Runa curtseyed as low as she could and kept her eyes firmly on the embroidered carpet at her feet.

Master Greigon seemed to have grasped the situation

and now stood, his mouth gaping like a goldfish that had jumped out of the pond.

"Ah, ah," he kept saying.

"Thank you, Master Greigon," King Mabrigas said coolly, losing none of his composure. "Consider yourself relieved of your duties. You will be paid for the full week."

"My King, you are most gracious." Greigon managed to say, before bowing and leaving.

Runa's legs ached from holding her curtsey for so long, but there was no way she was going to rise without her father's permission. She could feel his anger vibrating in the air, though he made no outward indication of it to the ambassador.

"Runa," the king said. "You will sit in the ante chamber until the good ambassador and I are finished."

"Yes, sire," she whispered.

Mistress Leira should have seen her. Runa paced out backwards, curtseying impeccably at the door, before walking erect and slow to the bench in the ante chamber beyond. She even remembered to sweep her skirts out so that they would not crease.

But there was no one to see her model behaviour. Mistress Leira was no doubt tapping her foot impatiently as she waited for her wayward pupil in the hall, and the page was too busy closing the doors and resuming his post. The guards seemed not to notice her, and the ante chamber was otherwise empty.

Runa sat as still as she could for as long as she could, but her feet soon started swinging, and as her heart slowed, her mind returned to her favourite subject, dragons. She could not quite forget the hard fist in the pit of her stomach however, and every time she heard the noise of a door or a footstep, it gave her a little squeeze, just to remind her of the trouble she was in.

Eventually, as the Day-Star began to dip low enough to flood the room with a rosy glow, Runa heard the squeak of her father's study door and then the soft pacing of the ambassador's slippered feet as he crossed the ante chamber, followed by his personal guard.

Runa was debating whether she should go to King Mabrigas and get it over with or wait and hope he had forgotten her when his voice rang out from his study.

"Runa!"

With a simmering feeling in her stomach, Runa got to her feet and walked reluctantly into her father's study. The heavy doors closed behind her, and she stood before him, her feet sinking into the thick pile of the rug before the fire, unable to raise her eyes to meet his.

"Runa," the disappointment was worse than his anger. "I know that things are difficult for you. Without a mother to guide you, your childhood has been harder than most. But you are my daughter, a princess of the realm of Feldemoore – the only princess. You cannot live as though your life is your own. You are thirteen now. It is time to put your childish ways behind you and stop living so selfishly.

"Our island is on the brink of war. Dark forces threaten to tear us apart. I was in delicate negotiations with the ambassador of Taranata. Your interruption was not only unspeakably rude but could have cost us an ally in a dangerous war."

Inside, Runa bubbled with rage. It was Master Greigon who had interrupted! She had wanted to stay outside!

"I have made up my mind. Tomorrow you will be escorted to Lelanta, to the school there. I suggest you go and pack your things."

Runa's eyes finally lifted off the floor and she stared at her father, aghast.

"To school? But ... but no! There are no dragons there!"

"You should have thought of that before you skipped lessons and refused to respect your tutors. I have had too many complaints."

"Father, please. I will study, I promise. I will do everything you say, anything, but please don't send me there!"

Runa's eyes filled with rare tears. The thought of being stuck indoors with a bunch of silly girls, all worrying about their hair and dresses and shoes ... and being forced to curl her hair and wear stockings and keep her clothes nice ... and worst of all – no dragons! Lelanta was a peaceful town, set in the gentler hills on the norther coast. It had no need of a military presence.

"You will spend a year there at least," King Mabrigas spoke firmly. Anger still glittered in his dark eyes and Runa's heart sank. "If you study hard and are willing to apply yourself to your own improvement then I might be persuaded to reconsider. But it is time you grew up, Runa. For too long I have let you run wild, without a good female influence. You are a young lady, a royal princess, but at the moment you are behaving like a hoyden."

For several heartbeats Runa stood on her father's rug, considering her best response. She could attempt tears, but they never came easily, and she ended up just looking like she was going to be sick. Anger was her more natural reaction, but the king's stony silence told her that a tantrum might just get her sent to Lelanta tonight instead of tomorrow.

"I have things to do, Runa," Mabrigas said at last, picking up a sheaf of papers.

Runa left silently, still in a state of shock. Surely Father would change his mind. But the hope simply would not rise. She knew her father. His sternness and firmness had made him a strong leader. His will, once fixed, would not easily be changed.

CHAPTER 3

In her bedroom, Runa kicked her bed and punched her pillows and screeched her rage into the curtains. It was not fair! She had not asked to be a princess! She would have been far happier in some peasant's cott, running after a herd of goats and raising chickens for a living. Let some other girl be a princess, one who liked dressing in silk and dancing and sitting still for endless hours through boring banquets.

Perhaps she could go and plead with Mareq; he might be willing to talk to Father for her. But then she remembered that he was away now, learning princely skills with one of father's governors. He was her closest brother in age, only fifteen, and they had been in the nursery together for a while when Runa was very young. The older two princes were proper adults now and had never had much to do with her; they had never seemed to want to.

It was at times like this that Runa most felt her lack of a mother. Surely a mother would understand and would speak to father, soften him a bit. A mother would offer comfort at least.

But Runa's mother had died when she was born. She had tried to feel sorry for herself, once in a while, for not having a mother, but with little success. Sometimes she felt a mother might have actually been a hindrance, for mothers usually cared more about things like keeping clothes nice, and hands clean, and sitting correctly. Father ignored those things or delegated them to tutors and governesses to whom Runa felt little obligation. Runa had watched other girls walking with their mothers around the palace, and they seemed happy enough. But for Runa, happiness was found in the dragon caves, and in climbing the orchard trees, in shooting for wild rabbits, and, on wet days, curling up with a book about dragon lore or perhaps the adventures of roaming sky riders or ancient stars. Stories about Elior were her favourite, even though he was from Callenlas to the south, and not Feldemoore.

Anyway, something had to be done, or she would be going to Lelanta in the morning.

Grabbing her bag, Runa put in it her favourite book, an apple left over from breakfast, and her sling. She changed into her brother's old tunic and hose, leaving

17

her dress crumpled on the floor. To her belt she strapped her mother's old paper knife that she had sharpened until it was as good as a dagger, then slipped out.

Runa's plan was, admittedly, lacking in clarity. Her shelves were stuffed with books by riders who had roamed the land, surviving in forests and building shelters, so she felt confident about spending a few nights in the forest, at least. Vaguely in the back of her mind was the hope that her father would miss her, come looking for her, and be so glad to see her again that he would never dream of sending her away to Lelanta.

The more reasonable part of her mind, which seemed to be growing more insistent and annoyingly sensible with each birthday, suggested that in fact running away would only land her in more trouble, but Runa was already planning her route out of the castle. It was about time she had a real adventure. She took the backstairs, ducking out of sight when servers passed on their errands, sneaking out through the laundry room instead of the kitchen. She was crossing the cobbled yard, aiming for the orchard, when she spotted the rows of carts standing in the courtyard.

Each day, farmers from the surrounding valleys brought cartloads of produce into the castle. The carts stood in the courtyard where servers could unload the baskets of vegetables, eggs, cheese and other food, and carry it into the kitchens for storing. The carts were almost certainly empty by now, waiting for their owners to come and drive them home.

Runa had lifted the cover of one cart and slipped into its cavity before the thoughts had fully slotted into place in her mind. She found herself in a cosy tent with a canvas roof and empty sacks to soften the bottom of the cart. Now all she had to do was make herself comfortable and wait.

Runa took out her book and began to read, but the evening Day-Star lay warm on the canvas overhead, and the sacks were actually pretty comfortable ... Runa found her eyes growing heavy.

ℝ ✱ ℞

Hunger woke her, and at first Runa could not remember where she was. It was dark and the cart beneath her was moving! The wheels creaked as they bumped over stones and ruts in the road, and Runa was gently rocking back and forth against the rough sacking.

Runa eased herself up, pushing her head through a gap in the canvas to peer out at a cold sky glittering with stars, the pointed tops of trees blocking their light at uneven intervals. The cart was travelling along a rough track leading down the side of the mountain, away from the castle. Looking behind her, Runa could even see its turrets, pointing darkly into the night, a few windows lit with lamps.

Runa craned her head and could see the dark hump of the driver in his seat, a lantern swinging near his head, its yellow light gleaming off the bald crown of the man's head.

The slow journey down the steep track gave her time to consider her next actions. The dense darkness of the forest, in spite of the stars and sliver of moon, was creeping into her consciousness. She was surprised by how cold the air was and was beginning to wish she had thought to bring a blanket. And some more food.

No, Runa told the panicking part of herself firmly. The whole point of this was to have an adventure and prove that she was worthy of training to be a sky rider. She had practised setting traps in the orchard – the fact that she had caught the cook's ginger tom cat only proved how successful she could be at animal trapping. She had to stay calm and think of a way to get off this cart unnoticed.

Runa thought about leaping out, but as she peered over the side of the cart, the ground seemed to be moving faster than she had expected. She would not want to sprain her ankle by landing awkwardly in the dark.

The howl of a wolf somewhere in the darkness sent a

shiver of fear down Runa's spine. The cart driver flicked his whip at the horse's rump and their speed increased slightly.

"I won't be afraid," Runa told herself firmly. The wolf's howl had been distant, and they usually kept well away from inhabited areas, especially in warmer weather. But perhaps it would be just as well to slip off the cart when it stopped and sleep near whatever village the driver lived in. Just in case.

ဆာ ✳ ಂ

The cart rattled to the foot of the mountain, then turned to the right, leaving the track and the trees to bump across a field of sheep. Soon they reached a low farmhouse. It was a single storey building with rather grubby whitewashed walls and a thatch roof. Firelight was spilling out of the window into the yard where the driver leaped down from his seat and began to unhitch the horse.

Runa decided now was the time to slip away, though she was disappointed to find the house stood alone in the middle of nowhere. She grabbed her bag and cloak and crept to the end of the cart. When the man led his old horse into the barn next to the house, Runa hopped off the end of the cart, intending to run for the trees.

"Who are you?" a loud voice demanded, sending Runa's heart leaping into her throat. Strong but soft arms wrapped around her from behind, and for a moment she was too startled to fight them. She was turned about to face a fractious looking woman with thin dark hair scraped messily into a bun and a face lined with discontent.

"I ... I fell asleep in your cart," Runa muttered.

"You from the palace?" the woman asked. Runa nodded.

The driver had now come out of the barn, a look of confusion on his face.

"You got a stowaway," the woman said to him. He seemed surprised in a vague, uncaring sort of way.

"You'll be in trouble," he observed.

"I suppose you'd better stay here," the woman sighed, raising her eyes, but releasing Runa. "You can go back with Ike tomorrow."

"Well, hang on," Ike complained, loudly. "I was supposed to go to Faradel tomorrow."

"You can set her as far as the road at least," the woman argued, pulling Runa towards the house.

Runa glanced over her shoulder at the forest. It seemed very dark now, for the moon was a bare sliver above the pointed tree-tops, and though the wolf was far away, she had heard they had a very good sense of smell.

From inside the little house wafted a delicious, savoury steam which made her mouth water. Her stomach gave a growl, and that decided it for her. Why stay out in the dark and cold when she could eat a hot meal and sleep within four walls? Then, in the morning, she could thank Ike for the lift and find a good place to build a shelter in the forest while it was daylight. She could even set a few traps and have a decent meal by the evening.

Yes, this was a much better plan. She followed the woman into the cottage.

Inside was a small room with a floor of beaten earth. A wide hearth held a crackling fire, and over it hung a pot – the source of the mouth-watering smell.

Near the fire stood a low wooden bench and a large table.

"I'm Morna," the woman was saying, moving to the shelf by the fire and taking down three thick, pottery plates. She ladled out spoonfuls of stew from the pot over the fire onto the plates, then clattered them down onto the table.

"This is Ike," she added, nodding at the man, who had already taken his spoon up. Runa gladly followed his example. There was bread too, coarser than Runa was used to, but tasty.

"I'm R... Reya," Runa said, remembering at the last

23

moment to change her name.

"And what is it you do, Reya?" Morna asked, her eyes fixed firmly on Runa. "At the palace."

Runa chewed and swallowed.

"I'm a housemaid," she said with a shrug. "I wash carpets, light fires. You know."

"You wash carpets?" Morna asked. Runa nodded.

"Sometimes I even clean the royal rooms," Runa continued, getting a bit carried away. She began to enjoy herself, now that food was in her belly and she was warming up. Maybe it would be fun to be someone else for a few hours.

But Morna was looking at Runa far too closely. Runa stretched her arms wide and gave an elaborate yawn.

"You've had a long day," Morna said. "You'll be wanting your bed, I expect."

Runa nodded, feigning weariness. She took up her bag and followed Morna from the table to a ladder which led up into a small loft. Morna put a sack over a bale of hay and patted it in a poor attempt at warmth.

"There you go," she said. "Sleep well."

Runa pantomimed a yawn and lay down upon the makeshift bed. After her sleep in the cart, she was far from tired, but she wanted to be away from Morna's beady, perceptive eyes.

Morna climbed down the ladder, taking the candle

with her, and Runa lay still for a while, listening to Morna moving around the room below, clearing away the plates. She and Ike discussed the price he had got for the meat and vegetables he had sold at the palace, and whether he would be taking wool to the market at the end of the week. Runa reached for her bag and took out her book, but then Morna's tone changed and Runa became alert.

"She's no server, that one," the woman said from her seat by the fire. "Servers don't wear clothes like that – did you see the stitching? She's a noble. Washing carpets indeed!"

Runa swallowed hard and cautiously inched her way off the mattress to press her eye to a gap in the floorboards. She could see the fire crackling in the wide hearth, Morna's hands picking with a needle at a shirt in her lap, Ike leaning back in his chair with his eyes half-closed, feet towards the flames.

As Runa watched, Morna turned her head to glance up at the attic where she thought Runa slept. There was a calculating expression on her face. She looked the way Runa had seen men looking at horses for sale, or women at silks for dressmaking. Runa's stomach turned over, and she lay as still as she could, holding her breath, wondering if her heartbeat could be heard through the boards.

Then Morna turned back to her mending and Runa released her breath slowly.

"She's worth a bit, that one," Morna whispered.

"What do you mean?" Ike growled, opening his eyes.

"She's healthy, strong. Good teeth. Fetch a good price."

"Come on Morna," Ike shook his head. "We're not flesh traders."

"You could tek her to Faradel tomorrow," Morna urged. "To Steer Street."

"No," Ike replied, but he seemed far from convinced. "If you're right, and she's noble, she'll have family. Someone'll miss her. We'll get into trouble. I'd rather be a poor free-man than a rich fool in prison."

Runa's heart was beating fast. She had to remind herself to breathe slowly or they might hear her against the boards.

"Who's going to find out once she's on a ship to Filios? Look, if you're worried, we can tek her cloak, put some blood on it from the mutton and tek it to the palace next week, say we found it in the woods. They'll think she was eaten by a wolf."

"I don't know, Morna," Ike sounded even more uncertain.

"Look," Morna dropped her sewing and leaned forward, her voice keen and stretched. "If you want to spend the rest of your life in this hovel, suit yerself. But I'm sick of bending and scraping while people like her live in comfort just 'cos she was born in the right place.

We're only getting what we deserve."

Ike was nodding in reluctant agreement.

"Tomorrow, we'll tek her to Faradel." Morna rose decisively and began putting out the lamps. Runa shifted, pressing her eye to the gaps between the floorboards, wondering how they secured the house. Ike lifted a heavy beam and laid it across the door. Morna closed the shutters with a bang and put bolts in place.

Runa's spirits sank. She was not going to get out of the windows – those bolts made too much noise; and the beam across the door was too heavy for her to lift. She would have to find an escape tomorrow, on her way to Faradel.

CHAPTER 4

Wirrat and Zaphreth had force-marched until Sarreia
was a thumbprint over the stars, resting on the lip of
the horizon. They were already further from home
than Zaphreth had ever been, and soon all he had ever
known would disappear below the rim of the earth. The
realisation gave him a lost sort of feeling, though he was
quick to choke it down and focus back on the road at his
feet.

At last, when Zaphreth felt his legs would soon give
way, Wirrat led Zaphreth off the road, into a clump of the
black grass.

"Start a fire, boy," he ordered, before stumping off
into the grass to relieve himself.

Inside, Zaphreth's resentment smoked, but tiredness
and hunger won over his pride and he bent to scrape
together a bundle of dried grass and twigs, shaking

28

them free of sand. He found quite a lot of dead wood lying around the base of some low, scrubby trees, and stacked it in a pyramid over the dead grass. The heat of the day had left the sand and the cold of a desert night was sinking into Zaphreth's bones. Tired and freezing, he had to concentrate hard to summon the energy required to start a fire, something that was usually easy for him. He Sent power from his fingers into the bundle of dried grass and the blue flames began to flicker, quickly turning to orange as the heat gathered. Zaphreth leaned back as the fire took hold and began laying bigger twigs until the fire was going well.

"That's better than flint and tinder," Wirrat muttered approvingly.

Zaphreth glanced up, startled. He had not heard the man approach.

"Trained in Mind Powers, then?" Wirrat asked, throwing himself down on a blanket, close to the fire.

Zaphreth nodded. It was not entirely true, but he didn't feel he owed this stranger an explanation.

"You're a quiet one and no mistake," Wirrat said, reaching into his pack. He brought out a packet of meat, some bread and a small flask. Stabbing the meat onto a couple of twigs, Wirrat set the slices over the flames before taking a swig from the flask. He passed it to Zaphreth.

"It'll warm you," Wirrat said.

Uneasily, Zaphreth took the flask and tried a small swig. He had drunk ale in the taverns, but this went down like fire and tasted like lamp oil. Zaphreth pulled a sour face and passed the flask back to Wirrat who laughed coldly and drank a second time. To be fair to Wirrat, the warmth of the drink in Zaphreth's empty stomach felt good and spread slowly to his fingers as he hunched and watched the meat sizzle.

As the flames grew and cast more light, Zaphreth allowed himself to take in more of Wirrat's appearance. His skin was very dark suggesting a life lived mostly outdoors, perhaps in the very southern parts of tSardia. The weathering and creases in his face hinted that he was older, perhaps sixty, but he moved and spoke with the energy of a much younger man. Those black eyes flicked up and caught Zaphreth watching. Wirrat's teeth flashed white as he grinned, or at least stretched his mouth wide; there was little warmth in the expression.

"So where do you hail from, Zaphreth?" Wirrat asked. "I'm from Dirisat, in the south, myself."

"I grew up near Sarreia, in one of the vineyard villages," Zaphreth said. "My father was chief vine tender for the prince."

A glimmer of sympathy registered in Wirrat's tough features, but Zaphreth turned away. He did not want sympathy.

He often said that he could only remember the desert, but it was not quite true. There was one memory that lingered, full of sweetness and green, of running between the vines, playing catch with the children of the other vine tenders. There were shrieks of delight, peeping eyes, and the flash of fabric as they ran and hid among the rows. Zaphreth had run his hands through soft, lush leaves on either side, his knuckles bumping gently against the swell of ripening grapes.

"Well, I'm turning in," Wirrat said gruffly, offended at Zaphreth's refusal to talk. He dug his blanket out of his pack and rolled himself in it, giving Zaphreth one last look with his black, glittering eyes.

"Watch out for scorpions," he said with a ghoulish grin, then scrunched his eyes shut, as firmly as if he'd closed a door on Zaphreth.

Slowly, Zaphreth pulled his blanket from his pack and unrolled it. He was nervous, suddenly, despite years of living in the desert. He had never slept out in the open. He scoured the darkened ground about the campfire for scorpions and snakes but found nothing.

Copying the more experienced traveller, Zaphreth wrapped himself in his blanket and used his pack as a pillow. He was weary to his bones, but sleep would not come. He did not fully trust his companion and kept hearing the rattle of scorpion feet against the sand. Twice he jumped up but found nothing.

Zaphreth looked up at the stars and exhaled slowly, trying to relax.

There was another memory, long hidden, of stealing handfuls of ripe fruit and eating them behind a harvest cart, the sweet juice dribbling down his chin. He had lied about it to his father, but the stains on his mouth had given him away, and he had been whipped for stealing the prince's fruit.

It was only a handful, Zaphreth had thought in his innocence, not realising that his father could have lost his job as chief vine tender if the prince's overseer found out. No one took anything belonging to Prince Lakesh.

The desert had put an end to it all anyway. Even as young as he was then, Zaphreth still remembered the worry in his parents' faces, the whispered conversations at night. The desert was expanding, creeping southwards across its breadth, eating up farmlands, villages, vineyards.

"Enchanted," some whispered, marking the sign against evil with their fingers. King Elior had cursed the ground, long ago, and the desert had been growing since.

"Nonsense!" Irek, his father, had roared, when Zaphreth suggested it one evening. "Children's fables. King Elior is a myth, perpetuated by the Callenlasians to keep fear in peoples' hearts and make them obedient. But we southerners, we are free! The tSardians know better than to believe in spirit stories. King Elior has no more power to curse land than I have to summon the wind."

Zaphreth had laughed with his father, but his mother, Ama, had remained silent and thoughtful.

By the time Zaphreth was seven, the vineyards were failing. Sand blew in from the north, corrupting the soil. The rains failed and Zaphreth worked with the other children, carrying water to pour along the bases of the vines. Still the fruit grew small and sour, and the overseer muttered about it being only good for vinegar, with a vinegary look on his face.

Families moved away. Father stayed on, stubbornly waiting for better times, but the day came when the last cart of sour grapes rattled its way along the road to Sarreia, and father closed up their house. It was the largest in the village, to fit his title as chief vine tender, with hand-painted tiles on the kitchen floor, Ama's pride and joy. Once a beautiful ilia plant had arched over the doorway, scattering the front courtyard with purple petals. The desert had taken that too, the rising heat too much for its delicate leaves.

Ama had wept all along the road, pulling her shawl over her head to hide her shame, though there was no one left to see it. Irek refused to be dispirited and sang as they walked to their new home. It barely deserved that name. It was a repurposed watchman's hut, built to guard the vineyards that had once lain like a striped blanket around the western side of Sarreia. Now the desiccated vines lay half-submerged in sand, like bleached bones. The only good things about their new house were that the rent was a pittance and it was nearer to the city, so that they could walk there every day to find work.

"Soon, we'll be able to afford a place in the city," Irek assured them as they sat miserably at their first meal in the new house. Its single room was barely the size of Zaphreth's old bedroom, and now he had to sleep on a shelf in the rafters. A 'mezzanine' Irek had called it proudly, but Zaphreth knew it was a shelf.

ဆာ ✱ လ

It was painful to remember all that had been lost to the desert; but it helped too. It reminded Zaphreth why he was sleeping in the open desert, so far away from home.

Zaphreth closed his eyes and drifted back to the evenings he had spent with his parents, so long ago now it seemed. Even before they moved to the watchman's hut, Irek had often spoken the histories of their people. But once they lost the vineyards and sat together in that single room, a little island in the expanse of sand, his father rehearsed the stories again and again.

"In the early days," he would begin, when the evening meal had been cleared away and the house had been shut up against the cold night air. "In the early days, the entire island of Callenlas was united under one king, a great and powerful warrior known as Elior. For generations there was peace, good trade across the sea, and prosperity.

"King Elior then travelled to other lands and established a line of human princes to rule our island. Callenlas was united for many generations, until Prince Arthen. Arthen preferred his younger son, Ilfian, and left the kingdom to him instead of tSardin, his eldest son. Angered at such injustice, tSardin raised an army from the people of the south. A great battle ensued, where men fought bravely and tSardin led with honour against his treacherous brother. Yet Ilfian was victorious and was crowned Prince of Callenlas after his father.

"Unwilling to submit to a usurper, Prince tSardin was himself crowned king over the south, in tSama. Many flooded to his lands, rejecting the rule of the false king of the north, and so our nation of tSardia was born.

"Here in the south, we have clung to reason and right rule. In the north they claim that their king is still Elior, that he returned two hundred years ago to reign over Callenlas again."

"But that's ridiculous, he would be hundreds of years

old!" Zaphreth protested, with a snort at the ignorance of the northerners.

"Exactly," Irek shook his son's shoulder in agreement. "They claim he is a star, come in the appearance of a man, and blessed with immeasurable years. But it's nonsense, of course. Each king is dressed in Elior's robes and pretends to be him; his legend is kept alive because it keeps the people in order, and in ignorance.

"For years, our two nations existed side by side, but now the time has come for the ancient wrongs to be put right, for the truth to be made plain. Our old king is weak and fearful, not so his heir. Prince Lakesh is gathering an army against the North. No longer will we ignore the injustice done to our fathers. No longer will we sit silent while Callenlas grows fat and wealthy on our lands. No longer will we allow a pretend king to reign over lands that should be ours.

"The days of petty skirmishes are over. War!" Irek brought his fist down on the little table with a crash, making Ama jump, and sending a thrill through Zaphreth's spine. He could see the horizon in Irek's eyes as his father watched the flames leap in the fireplace, rolling pistachios between his fingers before cracking the shells and tossing them into the hearth.

Every day they would all make the long walk to Sarreia, begging work from door to door, accepting ill-treatment for the sake of a few copper coins. Every day they would see the banners of Prince Lakesh's army fluttering in the breeze and watch the recruits march past in their crisp uniforms. A soldier commanded honour and a decent wage, and the drums of the past were calling to Irek's heart. He was used to having respect and authority over men. The four crumbling walls of the watchman's hut were too small for him; he reminded Zaphreth of the wild beasts caged for the prince's pleasure in the southern quarter of Sarreia.

The old king died that spring as hot winds from the south swept in, dragging the sand in great drifts against the little house. Lakesh was crowned in tSama, the southern capital, where the coastal air was cooler. Sarreia languished under the heat of a long summer. Irek mended roofs and doors and found Zaphreth an apprenticeship with a blacksmith.

News drifted from the south, carried by the merchants with their flat-footed camels dragging sand-sleighs full of silks and spices. The new king was building an army and looking for recruits. Skirmishes and raids were carried out against Callenlas, testing her mettle, finding her sleepy after years of peace.

Then Prince Lakesh appointed a new general, a master of war, who was pulling the army into shape, putting an end to petty raids. Sarreia was restless. The men gathered in taverns to talk, the women in clusters in the marketplace to worry. The apprentices talked too, tackling the sudden demand for swords and battle-axes with renewed zeal, eager to play their part in the unfolding of history, however small.

Then the General moved his headquarters to Sarreia, to be nearer the northern border. The whole city was turned upside down to accommodate him and his personal guard, as well as a new recruitment and training camp. But the citizens of Sarreia could hold their heads higher now. Their walls housed the General, the saviour of tSardia, the one who had led the charge at Hressa, and commanded the victory at Amreida.

Ama wept the day Irek came home in the grey uniform of a new recruit. But Zaphreth's heart swelled with pride, because at last something was being done to put right all that had gone wrong in their lives.

CHAPTER 5

As the walls and towers of Faradel came into view, Morna pushed Runa down among the sacks of grain and a basket of disgruntled chickens. Sacks were piled over Runa's head, and as her hands were tied and her mouth gagged, there was nothing she could do. Her mind had been racing all morning during the two-hour drive along bumpy mountain tracks, but now that they were on the smoother surface of the King's Highway, she still had no plan of escape.

Ike and Morna greeted the guards at the gatehouse and the cart rattled under the stone archway. Runa's muffled calls were drowned out by the wheels clattering over the drawbridge and cobbles. They turned this way and that, then the cart stopped.

The sacks were pulled away and Morna's face came in close to Runa's.

"Don't you dare make a sound," she hissed, showing Runa the gleaming blade of a meat knife. Runa shook her head, her eyes wide with real fear.

Morna removed Runa's gag and pulled her upright.

"Please," Runa whispered. "Please let me go. I won't tell anyone what you've done. I just want to go home."

"I've slaved for too long," Morna said shortly, "to have any pity on a hoity toity rich girl. You are my ticket to freedom, or at least to a house by the sea, what I've always wanted. Some nice clothes, soft white bread, and a girl to help me with the washing. Not much to ask, is it? I expect you've had your bread buttered for you all your life, hain'tcher?"

Runa was pushed roughly to the edge of the cart. With her hands tied, the jump was too high, so Ike guided her down with a grunt.

He turned back to help Morna, and Runa saw her chance.

They were in a narrow alleyway, so Runa ducked out of it straight away and sprinted along the street. She wanted to find a place with lots of people, and then someone official to help her, but she had only visited Faradel once or twice, and of course had never been permitted to wander the streets – she had no way of knowing where to go.

Her feet slammed into the cobbles, behind her she

could hear Ike spluttering and Morna shrieking with rage. Runa turned a corner and heard Ike stumble at the rapid change of direction.

This street was wider, which gave her some hope. She noticed she was running uphill and a fact she had picked up somehow from one of her tutors surfaced in her mind: Feldemoore's cities always had the Governor's house at the highest point. All streets led upwards to it.

Keep going up, Runa told herself, as her chest burned and her feet hurt. It was hard to run with her hands tied, hard to keep her balance as she ducked and weaved.

Then she found a bustling market square and gained some ground. Winding through stalls and people, Ike struggled to keep up. Glancing behind her, his face was purple, his eyes bulging as he tried to keep pace.

As the sounds of the market fell behind her, Runa's chest burned and she knew she could not run much further. But there – she could see the gold tips on the towers of a great house, signifying an official dwelling, the dark orange flags of Feldemoore fluttering against the blue sky. It must be the Governor's house.

Runa thudded on the door, leaning against the timbers as she fought for breath.

"Who goes there?" called a lazy voice.

Ike had rounded the corner and was staggering up the hill after her.

"Let me in! I seek refuge!" Runa cried desperately.

"Who goes there?" the voice repeated, with irritation.

"I am the Princess Runa! Open in the name of the King!"

Ike's dirty hand was reaching for her, but the bolt was being drawn back, iron grating against iron. The door opened and Runa all but fell over the threshold. She pointed with her bound hands and threw out her accusation in a loud voice.

"That man was going to sell me to flesh traders!"

Ike's face dropped with horror as he realised where he was. He scrabbled backwards and ran.

"After him!" Runa urged the pair of dumbfounded guards who stood about the dim entrance. They glanced at each other, then set off after Ike at a half-hearted trot.

Runa did not care whether they caught him or not. She was safe. She almost cried, lying there on the cool tiles of the Governor's back entrance. But future sky riders don't cry.

Runa hauled herself to her feet, still out of breath, and faced the gatekeeper. He was a small, mousy man, slightly hunched, with twitchy eyes.

"Please, take me to the Governor," Runa said, in her best princess voice.

The gatekeeper narrowed his eyes.

"Why would he want to see you?"

"I am the Princess Runa!"

Runa suddenly realised that she might not exactly look like a princess. She was wearing Mareq's old tunic and hose, had spent a night in an attic and several hours in a dirty cart. Chicken feathers poked out of the tunic in places, along with a few well-placed straws. She was red in the face and sweating from running. It was the longest she had ever managed to escape having her hair brushed.

Swallowing hard, Runa altered her posture and tried to smooth down her hair (a difficult task with tied hands). She held out her wrists to the doorman.

"At least untie me," she said.

The doorkeeper produced a small knife from his belt and hacked at the ropes. He then led Runa to an ante chamber, pleasantly cool with windows looking over a small courtyard.

"Wait here, please," the doorkeeper shuffled away while Runa took a seat on a padded bench. There was a fountain in the courtyard, and at once the tinkling of water made her feel more at ease. Runa drew a deep breath and exhaled, waiting for her legs to stop trembling and for the unpleasant feeling of having had a very narrow escape to subside.

After a short while a tall man entered the room, followed by two armed guards and the shuffling doorman.

"Uncle Izzecha!" Runa exclaimed, hopping off the bench.

"It is you!" Uncle Izzecha drew Runa into a tight embrace and for a moment she allowed herself to feel small and protected.

"What are you doing here?" Uncle Izzecha bent down to look into Runa's eyes. Of her three uncles, Izzecha was her favourite. Father's youngest brother, he rarely visited court, but when he did, he always made time for Runa. He dressed well too, today in a long robe of navy, that cleverly shifted to a deep purple in the light. His hair was dark blond, his beard neatly trimmed and he smelt pleasantly of pine and sandalwood. Around his neck hung a long chain, with a pendant of vivid sapphire that caught the light on its surfaces, while beneath lay depths of dark blue.

"You have been having adventures, haven't you?" He chuckled, plucking a piece of straw from Runa's hair.

"I was kidnapped!" Runa shuddered. "They were going to sell me to flesh traders."

For the time being she chose to leave out the part about hiding in the cart of her own volition, as well as her hope of scaring her father, though her guilt had been growing overnight.

Uncle Izzecha frowned.

"You know the flesh trade is outlawed in Feldemoore."

44

"Well, they knew someone." Runa hugged herself tightly, suddenly absorbing the horror she might have been subjected to.

"Look at you," Uncle Izzecha put his arm around Runa's shoulders. "You need a hot bath and some food."

A bath had never sounded so good. Runa was led upstairs to one of the large guest rooms. Food was quickly procured, hot water fetched, and a bath filled. Runa sank into the tub with a sigh and felt the warmth soothing her limbs. A dress was found for her, too frilly and pink for her liking, but it was clean and only slightly too big.

"Shall I burn these?" the maid asked, tentatively picking up Runa's discarded tunic and hose.

"No!" Runa exclaimed. "Please wash them and bring them back to me."

The maid raised a doubtful eyebrow but had little choice but to obey the Princess of Feldemoore.

Runa looked at herself in the mirror. Her hair was straight and coppery, and she wished she was permitted to keep it shorter, but at least it went well enough with her eyes, which were green. A smattering of freckles coloured the bridge of her nose, which most girls would disdain, but Runa, in her usual contrariness, liked. No one would ever call her a beauty, but she had never minded that much. What made her heart swell was when her brothers complimented her aim with a bow, or when she could keep her balance longest on a log over a stream.

What was she going to do at Lelanta?

CHAPTER 6

Zaphreth woke stiff and cold, the fire a heap of ash that drifted in the desert wind. The morning was already hot, and the shimmering desert obscured Zaphreth's final view of Sarreia.

Wirrat was nowhere to be seen and Zaphreth felt a moment of panic, before he realised that his guide's pack still sat on the other side of the fire.

Watching the long, spidery shadows cast behind the grass by the Day-Star's early light, feeling the contrast of cool sand and the Day-Star's warmth, Zaphreth could not help remembering a very similar morning, barely a year ago.

Standing in the doorway of the hut, Zaphreth had been looking along the road to the city, watching it dance in the heat even though it was long before noon. He had been thinking about the last day he had seen his father.

Irek had kissed Ama, shouldered his pack and walked until he was nothing more than a grey smudge against the dust. Ama had wept, while Zaphreth's chest burned with pride.

"Close the door," Ama called from inside, for the warm wind whipped up the ochre dust, driving it into the little house.

Zaphreth ignored her and remained looking along the road. He'd lost count of the days that had passed since his father had gone. Usually it was empty, a barren track heading north to join the main road to Sarreia. Today a figure appeared, a dark smudge against the clouds of dust. Too tall and too bulky to be anything but a traveller on horseback.

It was a mounted officer, Zaphreth realised with a chill, as the horse came within clear sight. The single feather in his helm marked him out as a commander of a hundred. An officer in the service of the General.

Zaphreth stood rooted to the spot.

Let him be lost. Let him be lost, he thought, though he knew with gut-clenching certainty that the soldier was not lost. No one came this way unless they meant to.

The commander drew in his horse outside the house. Even coated in a film of dust, he was an awe-inspiring figure. His black uniform was crisply pressed, his buckles gleamed in the Day-Star's light.

"Is this the dwelling of Irek of Havara?"

Zaphreth swallowed. It felt as though all the dust of tSardia was choking up his throat.

"It is, sir," he replied.

The commander dismounted, his sword and buckles clinking. The horse stood still, trained to perfection.

"Is the mistress here?"

Zaphreth nodded.

"Will you take me to her?" the rider asked with an edge of impatience.

Ama was inside winding up balls of yarn to sell door to door in the city. Zaphreth led the rider within; he removed his helm but still had to duck under the door frame.

Ama's dark eyes rose from the table to their visitor. Her face turned grey. She crumpled.

"Take courage," the commander said gently to her, catching her in his arms. "He is not dead."

To Zaphreth he said, "Do you have any spirits in the house?"

Zaphreth indicated the bare walls and shelves with his hands.

"Then fetch water. Cool, from the well."

Zaphreth ran. The well was at the back of the house. He dropped the bucket down and heard the echoing splash. He filled a cup and carried it back into the house.

Ama was still cradled in the soldier's arms, he held her as gently as a child. He took the cup from Zaphreth, who stood helpless while the commander coaxed Ama to sip slowly. Gradually she revived, and the stranger helped her sit on the small stool near the fire, where her bakestone was still heating on the coals.

"He's not dead?" Ama gripped the commander's hands, clutching for hope.

"No."

"Then why have you come?" Ama spoke with a weary bitterness, turning her head aside to look out of the small, square window into the desert.

"Irek of Havara quitted himself well of his duties to the General, commander of the armies of tSardia," the soldier used formal language, but his tone was gentle. "I was his commander, leading him at the siege of Canvara. He was always obedient, always hard working."

Ama nodded, recognising her husband in his words. She had a strange smile on her face, polite, and at odds with the lost focus of her eyes.

"We sought to attack Canvara and succeeded in bringing down part of the wall," the commander went on. "But they had more men than we anticipated and drove us back, breaking out of the city to swarm around us. They slaughtered some and captured many."

"So, he is a prisoner?" Zaphreth asked. His fists were

clenched in two tight balls of anger.

The commander nodded gravely.

"When was he taken?" Ama's voice croaked.

"The siege was broken two weeks ago. I recovered as many of my men as I could and we returned to the main camp. I am on a week's leave but I wanted to deliver the news to you in person. Irek spoke so often of you, and of his son, that I could not let a stranger bring this message to you."

Ama pressed his hands tightly until her knuckles turned white.

"Let me make some food for you," she said.

"No, no. You need not trouble yourself."

The commander stood, his frame filling the tiny room. Ama seemed small and pathetic in his shadow.

Zaphreth followed him out to his horse, watched as the soldier untethered the magnificent animal and prepared to mount up. He did not want to ask, but had to.

"What do they do to prisoners of war?"

The commander hesitated, one hand on the horse's bridle. He looked down at his feet in the dust.

Slowly, he turned his head to look at Zaphreth.

"We do not know," he admitted. "They have returned none, in spite of our negotiations."

"Do they execute them?"

"It is against their laws."

"Torture?"

A sickening pause, while Zaphreth clenched his fists until his nails drew blood.

"We do not know."

Zaphreth stared at the commander, his pristine uniform worth a month's wages, if not more. Zaphreth's muscles twitched with restrained rage.

"So what do we do now?" he asked, with a shrug. "We have not been sent father's wages for three months."

The commander sighed.

"I will speak with the quarter-master of my battalion," he said, while loosening a purse from his belt. "In the meantime, take this."

The purse lay heavy in Zaphreth's hand, blood money.

"How old are you?" the commander asked.

"Thirteen," Zaphreth replied.

"When you are fourteen, enlist. Serve in the armies of the General and help us rid ourselves of the pestilence in the North. When we are free of the tyranny of King Elior, then we will have peace."

Zaphreth watched as the commander mounted up and turned his horse, riding back to Sarreia along the dusty road.

CHAPTER 7

It was hard to shake his sense of desolation even when Wirrat stumped noisily to the fire and hoisted his pack up.

"Enjoy your lie-in?" he asked, irritable.

Zaphreth picked himself up and shook out his blanket.

"No time for daydreaming, boy," Wirrat said before sauntering off to the road without a backward glance.

Zaphreth rolled up his blanket in haste, stuffing things into his pack and running to catch up with his guide. He wondered who exactly Wirrat was. He had assumed he was a soldier, but he wore no badge or token to indicate his rank or commander. But then, Zaphreth supposed, neither did he. This was a secret mission so he was dressed as he had been before he joined the army, as a poor apprentice.

"Where did you learn your mind tricks, then?" Wirrat

asked, after a while. He had apparently forgiven Zaphreth for sleeping in and daydreaming.

"I didn't learn, exactly," Zaphreth said, unsure of how much to reveal. "I used to move my toys as a child, and when my parents taught me how to make fire and light, I found it easy."

Wirrat whistled.

"Are you a descendant of stars, then?" he asked.

Zaphreth looked at Wirrat keenly.

"Don't tell me you believe those stories?" he scorned.

Wirrat chuckled mirthlessly.

"I've seen stranger things than walking stars, boy," he said. "When you've travelled as much as I have and seen as much as I have, you realise anything might be true."

Zaphreth mused on Wirrat's words, troubled that someone in the service of Lord Lur might believe such silliness.

"When did you enter the General's service?" Zaphreth decided to do some probing of his own.

Wirrat laughed his flat, mirthless laugh.

"I serve no one, boy, understand that," he said. "No one except Wirrat, that is."

Zaphreth frowned again, perturbed by such anarchy. A flicker of anxiety pattered in his chest as he wondered why the General would choose such a mercenary to do important work. But then Zaphreth calmed himself, reminding himself that Wirrat's job was not that important. Zaphreth, had the real mission, the real work to do. Wirrat was just a guide. What he thought mattered little.

80 ✳ ဂ8

On the fourth day they left the road and began crossing the desert using only Wirrat's judgement and the Day-Star's position to guide them. They were heading north-east, slogging across the drifting sand. A wind had come up from the north, blowing dust into their faces. Off the packed surface of the road the sand was slippery and hard to walk on, and they covered ground very slowly.

Wirrat called a halt in the mid-afternoon and they dropped into the shelter of a small cluster of thorn bushes. It was too windy to light a fire, so they slept, their blankets over their heads to keep off the worst of the sand.

Wirrat shook Zaphreth awake when the Day-Star was barely a sliver of light in the east, the western horizon still lost in shadow. The wind had died overnight, and the morning was still and cool.

"Look," Wirrat said, pointing to the north. "The patrols are on their way out. That's the main Callenlasian camp there, two miles that way."

As they watched, large, angular shadows left the

55

greater darkness of the ground and rose unevenly, like massive, ungainly birds into the sky. Dragons, Zaphreth realised with a shudder, used by the army to patrol the borders. They were also a formidable weapon in battle, for red dragons could scorch the enemy while the blacks could snatch up soldiers and carry them high into the air to dash them to the ground.

"Have you ever seen one, up close?" Zaphreth asked in a whisper, though there was no one around for miles.

"A dragon? A few times," Wirrat replied. His eyes were riveted on the spectacle as ten, eleven, twelve of the massive blacks rose from the camp and began sweeping across the land in different directions. It was the first time Zaphreth had seen anything other than cynicism in his guide's weathered face, and it made Wirrat seem a bit less prickly.

Still, dragons gave Zaphreth the shivers. He pressed himself back into the grass as one passed by overhead, its rider a small hump on its great back, scouting the ground only seventy paces above them. The vast wings made a rippling shadow on the dunes, and when it flapped to gain height, the sand and grasses beneath gusted as if a strong wind was blowing.

Wirrat watched the dragon pass and fly unevenly towards the south, before searching in his pack for some breakfast.

"Do your magic," he nodded to Zaphreth.

Zaphreth sighed, partly at Wirrat's laziness but also at the very common misunderstanding of Mind Powers. It looked like magic, but anyone could learn to do it. It was simply sending the natural power of the body beyond the physical restraints of muscles and joints and skin. Magic was another thing entirely.

Still, the fire felt good in the early morning cold, and better still was the smell of frying strips of rabbit meat. The meat was tough and sinewy but salty and delicious on a cold morning when Zaphreth had nothing else inside him.

"So how did a youngster like you end up in the service of the great General himself?" Wirrat asked, with no small touch of irony, leaning back to let his meal settle. He picked at the crumbs of oatcake scattered over his tunic. Zaphreth shifted his body to find a more comfortable position on the sand. He was growing more used to Wirrat's unpredictability. If his guide was in a more investigative mood, Zaphreth needed to humour him for as long as he could.

"I signed up as a regular recruit on my fourteenth birthday," Zaphreth said, recalling the morning. Ama had scraped some coppers together to buy a meal of goat's meat and spices, fried over the fire. Zaphreth had eaten hastily, eager to get into Sarreia and put his name down.

Ama watched him with anxious eyes, and Zaphreth knew she wanted him to linger. She wanted to hold onto her boy for a few hours longer. But he was a man now. She had to let him go.

Walking into Sarreia, Zaphreth held his head high. It was a new feeling, a good feeling, and his stride was light. Today, his name would be on the roster for the army of King Lakesh. He would be issued with a crisp, new uniform with gleaming buckles and a belt for a sword. He would have silver jingling against his hip, admiring glances from the girls at the stalls, and instead of eyeing him with suspicion and searching his bag, the guards would salute him and stand to attention.

Ambition burned in Zaphreth's breast as he made his way, not to Artem's ramshackle forge in a forgotten corner of the city, but to the official buildings at the centre. A troop of soldiers passed him on the way, marching in unison, heads raised, and all the people made way for them. Zaphreth watched them, his eyes bright. He would be one of them soon, with the king's emblem on his breast, marching under the navy banner. He would fight for justice, for the rights of his people. Visions of himself slicing through the enemy, planting the flag on a newly conquered town, rising through the ranks to fight alongside the generals and even the king himself ran through Zaphreth's mind in glorious colour. He walked faster.

The doors of the army headquarters were cut of black stone, engraved with a relief of past victories against Callenlas, and the Druseian pirates who sometimes attacked the southern coastal cities. Perhaps a relief would be carved of himself, Zaphreth thought, when he had proved himself in the ranks. He would bring his mother and show her. She would be grateful then, when she could hold her head high among the women of Sarreia. When they had a nice house with a pillared veranda and a whole garden of ilia flowers.

The guards halted him before he had even stepped over the threshold.

"What do you want, boy?" one of them asked, waving his spear at Zaphreth's chest. Zaphreth sighed; he had forgotten his rough apprentice clothes. But the guard wore green; he was only a city guard. Soon, Zaphreth would be above him, in the grey of a novice in the King's Guard.

"I am here to sign up," he said, his voice calm.

The guards laughed.

"They don't want boys, only men."

"I come of age today."

More laughter.

"Go on then," one of the guards chuckled, lowering his spear but aiming a cuff at Zaphreth's head. "See what they say to you."

Zaphreth hurried in, shrugging his shoulders to shake off the guards' laughter. He straightened his tunic, lifted his head, and walked to the desk on the right, where a scribe was sitting. His robes were the colours of the King's Guard but they were faded and dusty. This was no warrior, just a servant of the army. He scribbled noisily, absorbed in the papers scattered across his table.

Zaphreth cleared his throat. The scribe peered up at him through short-sighted eyes.

"Yes?" he asked, in a reedy voice, frustrated at being disturbed.

"I am here to sign up."

The scribe blinked and looked at Zaphreth again.

"For the King's Guard."

Still no response.

"For the war. I want to fight."

"Yes, yes," the scribe shuffled his papers about on his desk. "You seem very young."

"I come of age today," Zaphreth asserted, trying to stand taller. He knew he was small for his age, but there had never been enough food. "I am fourteen. I am strong."

"No doubt, no doubt," the scribe at last found the paper he wanted and spread it out on the desk, pressing out the creases. "Name?"

"Zaphreth son of Irek, of ..." he had been going to say 'Havara', the village he had grown up in, but that was left to the ghosts and the desert now. "Of Sarreia," he concluded.

The scribe scribbled away with his quill.

"And you are fourteen, you say?"

"I am."

"Hmm. You are sure you don't want to wait a year or two? Most boys are sixteen or seventeen before they sign up."

"I want to fight," Zaphreth repeated. "They have captured my father. I want to destroy Callenlas."

The scribe nodded wearily.

"Very well, very well. Take this —" he held out a note on a small sheet of paper, "and go to the back door of the barracks."

Zaphreth took the note between his fingers. The scribe was shuffling through his papers once more. Zaphreth had expected more ceremony, more gratitude for his willingness to serve, more recognition for his willingness to fight and die. But this was just a scribe, who had probably never seen a day's battle. He could not know the glory of fighting for one's country.

Zaphreth followed the lanes around to the barracks and knocked on a small door in the wall. A servant admitted him, and led him through some back rooms, past an open court where some twenty boys were running through some sword drills – *that'll be me, soon*, thought Zaphreth – and on through the barracks to a small ante room. The bare walls were lined with benches, and a collection of boys sat there, waiting.

"Wait here," his guide told him. There were no seats left on the benches, so Zaphreth stood with one or two others, unsure of what he was waiting for. Some of the boys were twice his size, seventeen and eighteen-year-olds whose legs sprawled across the flagstones. One or two appeared closer to his age, which gave him hope, and one boy sat silently in the corner, tears dripping down his face.

The boys shuffled as they waited, scuffing the floor with their sandaled feet. Most kept their eyes down, but one, a broad-shouldered, sandy-haired youth of at least eighteen, sat upright on the bench, looking at each boy in turn as though assessing them. When he came to Zaphreth, Zaphreth folded his arms and looked directly back, meeting his eye. Did he think he was better than everyone else because he wore a purple tunic and leather shoes?

"What are you looking at, scum?" the boy threw at Zaphreth when he refused to drop his eyes.

Zaphreth held his gaze for a moment longer, ignoring the trembling he felt inside, then coolly looked away to the window.

He had seen people shaped by their poverty, like Ama,

slowly becoming thinner, greyer, until they accepted being less than nothing. That was not going to happen to him. Like Irek, he was going to fight.

The door at the far end of the room opened and a stooped man with a tasselled hat and faded scholars' robes beckoned them in. He had a kind face. Zaphreth, who had been expecting a military man, felt curious and slightly relieved. Perhaps this would not be as painful as he had anticipated.

"I am Master Filias. I'll be assisting in your assessment today. Get in line please boys, ready to come through."

Most of the boys stepped willingly into line, but the large boy, who had confronted Zaphreth, shoved others aside to join the head of the line.

"Watch it, country boy," he said to Zaphreth. "Get to the back, where you belong."

Smouldering inside, Zaphreth clenched his fists, and took a place in the line further back. They were led into a long, low hall, with sanded, unvarnished boards. A stack of shields, swords and staffs cluttered the wall at the far end. Tall, narrow windows admitted light through one of the whitewashed plaster walls.

At the end of the hall, joined by the shuffling man in Masters' robes, stood an army commander, wearing the silver-edged cloak of a ruler of five hundred. His face looked as if it had been chiselled from rock. His narrow

63

gaze swept over the straggling line of boys, but his craggy features gave away nothing.

Zaphreth glanced along the straggling line of boys, worrying about the impression he would make upon the commander. He was easily the worst dressed, with his simple, undyed tunic, the edges frayed, and the fabric smudged with soot from the blacksmith's workshop. Ama had washed it, beating the dirt out and hanging it in the Day-Star's light, but the soot had worked into the fibres of the linen, and nothing would remove it.

Soon they would be issued with uniforms, he told himself, and then there would be no distinction. Except perhaps in size, for he also realised that he was among the youngest and smallest of the new recruits.

The morning passed quickly, in a series of tests. The boys were asked to run up and down the length of the hall several times, to see who tired quickly. Zaphreth held out over six or so of the other boys, but then he had to rest. The boy in the purple tunic kept going until the commander told him to stop, and even then, he was barely winded.

"Impressive, Eldor," the commander commented, making a note on the parchment before him.

They were then sorted into three groups according to how much experience they had with weapons. Only a handful of the boys were already well trained; most had some experience. Zaphreth joined the group of boys with no experience at all. The commander was pleased with Zaphreth's grip on the sword – a lesson he had learned early in the blacksmith's workshop – but the drills they were taught were entirely new to him.

The more experienced boys watched the lowest group from the other side of the hall, while waiting their turn to spar. They sniggered at the mistakes they made, and when Zaphreth dropped his sword Eldor laughed outright.

All of Zaphreth's pride swelled in his breast. *At least I'm trying*, he wanted to yell. He wanted to punch Eldor in the face but didn't think he could reach. *One day*, he comforted himself, *one day I'll be your commander.*

After a similar exercise with bows and blunted arrows, the boys were invited to go to another room where some food had been laid out for them. Zaphreth's mouth watered at the plates of fruit, soft bread, and cold meat that filled the trestle table, but once again, Eldor decided who should access the table first, pushing into the line.

"Couldn't they have had separate recruitment rooms for the stronger sort?" he asked one of his companions in a loud voice.

Zaphreth had enough. He stepped out of the line and pushed in front of Eldor, taking up a wooden plate.

"Hey!" Eldor shoved Zaphreth's shoulder. "Who do you think you are? Go to the back, slum-boy."

Zaphreth ignored him and put a slice of cold pork onto his plate.

"Did you hear me, scum? I don't want you touching my food with your grubby hands."

Another shove. Zaphreth picked up a loaf of bread.

"I don't even know what you're doing here; a whelp like you will only get in the way on the frontline. Perhaps they'll put you to digging cess-pits — that's what you're used to, isn't it?"

Some of the other boys sniggered.

"I bet his mother is a floor-sweeper."

Enough.

Zaphreth picked up his slice of pork, whirled and threw it into Eldor's face. It stuck, for a moment, then slowly unpeeled to smack on the wooden boards. A stunned silence filled the room, then Eldor stepped forward, towering over Zaphreth.

"Fool," he hissed, disdain flaring his nostrils, anger twisting his mouth. He put his hand around the back of Zaphreth's neck and began pushing down. The boys around them broke into shouts and cheers. Under the bigger boy's strength Zaphreth strained but had no hope. He was pressed against the floor. His plate clattered, an apple bumping and rolling across the boards.

Rage boiled within him. Zaphreth drew back his hand and threw out power with all his strength.

Eldor flew across the room, scattering tables and benches and hitting the wall with a sickening thud. He slumped down onto the floor and lay still.

The boys stopped cheering. Zaphreth picked himself up painfully – using his power like that always left him drained. He had only done it once or twice, in the desert by himself, to see what would happen. The other boys were staring at him and Zaphreth realised they were afraid.

A door creaked and Master Filias pattered in, drawn by the initial noise of the fight. He took in the scene quickly, the scattered chairs, the reduced Eldor now groaning as he returned to consciousness.

"What happened here?" Master Filias asked, quietly. His reserve made Zaphreth nervous. Now that he was calming down, he was beginning to think through what this could mean – rejection from the army? Perhaps imprisonment or public punishment if Eldor's family were important. Zaphreth swallowed hard.

"That boy shoved Eldor across the room," one of Eldor's cronies pointed his finger at Zaphreth.

A clamour arose among the boys. To Zaphreth's amazement, some of them were defending him, protesting that Eldor had provoked him.

"He didn't shove him, numbskull," one of the older boys corrected the first, raising his voice over the others. "He used Mind Powers."

There was a trace of awe in his voice, leaving Zaphreth more uncomfortable than ever.

Master Filias looked at him with a newly sharpened gaze, all the vagueness gone.

"Help Eldor up and take him to the infirmary. Explain that he was struck with a mind's force."

Two boys hurried over to the dazed Eldor.

"I think you had better come with me," Master Filias said to Zaphreth.

Zaphreth's stomach tightened. What would they do to him now? Would he be relegated to sweeping the streets for the rest of his life? Could they take his apprenticeship from him? Wild thoughts raced through Zaphreth's mind, supreme over all a wail of injustice. His hope of escape from poverty and misery was being snatched from him before it had even begun.

Master Filias led him through the barracks to a small door of heavy wood. He fumbled for a key in his robes, then unlocked the door and let Zaphreth inside. The Master quickly closed the door behind him and locked it again.

"This way," he said, leading Zaphreth along a narrow, dim passage. At one point, Filias lit his palm, for the only light came from an occasional lamp set into the walls, and some had gone out.

At last, the passage opened out onto a small ante-chamber with polished wooden benches against the walls. The massive stones of the walls were covered in places by expensive tapestries. Two windows, well above head-height, admitted daylight making Zaphreth blink after the long passage.

"Wait here," Master Filias said. He left by one of the doors and Zaphreth was alone.

He rubbed his hands together and wondered if he should go back down the passage and look for a way out. There had been several doors in the left wall, perhaps one of them was an escape. Perhaps he could open the lock using his powers. It would be tricky since he could not see inside the lock, but he might manage it. He and Ama could go to the coast and start again. It was not what he wanted, but it was better than being in prison, or publicly whipped.

He wondered whether Eldor had broken any bones. He hoped not. Well, a part of him hoped he had, but most of him now hoped he was just a bit dazed from hitting his head. The crunch of his body against the plaster had been horrible. *He deserved it*, thought Zaphreth, though he wished he had not used quite so much force now. His anger had made the expulsion of power stronger than usual.

Zaphreth waited and waited. Twice he set off down the dark corridor, intending to try the lock and escape. But he then remembered that the door opened onto the barracks, and if Master Filias came back and found him gone, half of the King's Guard would be after him. There was nothing he could do but wait and hope that whoever dealt with him would be merciful. Master Filias seemed fair, though Zaphreth's experience of life told him that his poverty made him the object of suspicion before he even opened his mouth. In most people's eyes he was already a thief and a wastrel.

The door creaked at last and Master Filias's unfocused blue eyes peered into the room.

"Will you come with me, please?" he said.

Zaphreth rose, wiping his sweating palms on the skirt of his tunic. He was led by the Master through a series of rooms, each one beautifully furnished, often with painted and gilded friezes on the walls and expensive carpet underfoot, but Zaphreth barely noticed. His heart was pounding now, his stomach in knots.

"Who instructed you in Mind Powers?" Master Filias asked as they walked.

"Uh, my parents," Zaphreth replied, though they had hardly instructed him at all. They had shown him how to light his palm, how to start fires and light lamps, but Zaphreth had discovered the rest by himself.

"Your parents?" Master Filias looked back at his paper. "Vine tenders?"

"My father was Master of the prince's vineyards, before the desert took them. Now he is a foot-soldier in the King's Guard."

Master Filias, glancing back, peered at Zaphreth again with narrowed eyes.

"Do you have any siblings?"

"No."

"Your grandparents?"

"I think they worked the vineyards too, but they're all dead now." Zaphreth wondered why Master Filias was so interested in his family, but they drew to a halt at an archway into another passage.

"The king's General wishes to see you," Master Filias said.

Zaphreth's stomach turned over, and he stared at Master Filias.

"Why would he bother with me?" Zaphreth asked in a small voice. "Couldn't the city governor just deal with me?"

"Deal with you ...?" Master Filias scratched the tip of his nose with his quill, leaving a smudge of ink.

"Punish me. For attacking Eldor. I don't mind a whipping but please don't take my apprenticeship. If I can't be in the army ... I need some way of earning a living." The words

71

tumbled out of Zaphreth's mouth, carrying all the anxiety that had built up while he waited. He despised his begging voice. This was what poverty did to a person, he thought. Reduced them to miserable, pleading dependence.

"Tut tut. You are not in trouble!" Master Filias patted Zaphreth's forearm then drew his hand back. "Dear me! Were you waiting all that time? Oh dear! You are not in trouble, my boy. To the contrary. The king's General is looking for those who show strength in Mind Powers. He wishes to interview you."

Zaphreth wanted to sit down. He could hear the blood pounding in his ears, feel heat in his cheeks. He was not in trouble. The relief of that alone would make him dizzy. But King Lakesh's General wanted to see him? Zaphreth's legs shook as he followed Master Filias along the low passage.

෨ * ෬

It was impossible to explain all this to Wirrat, so Zaphreth summarised.

"The masters noticed I had skill in Mind Powers, so they brought me to the General."

Wirrat nodded, accepting the brief answer.

"What about you?" Zaphreth ventured. "Are you in the army? Or a servant of the General?"

Wirrat's mouth curled in a cruel smile that made Zaphreth clench his toes. His guide kicked sand over the fire and reached for his pack.

"I told you already, boy," Wirrat said. "I answer to nobody but myself. Give me enough money and I'll do your dirty work, but I'm my own master."

Zaphreth licked his lips but had little time to worry. Wirrat was already rolling up his bed and fastening his pack. In the wilderness, Zaphreth knew he had to stay close to his guide. He gathered his things and prepared for another long day of walking.

CHAPTER 8

Uncle Izzecha's blue eyes danced with merriment as he leaned over his large desk, pushing a silver tray of sweets towards Runa. She was feeling much better after a good night's sleep and breakfast, though there was still a fist of anxiety in her stomach that clenched whenever she thought of Lelanta

"Well," said Uncle Izzecha. "You have been leading my brother a merry dance, haven't you?"

Runa gave a rueful shrug and helped herself to a raisin cake spiced with cloves. Honey glistened on the top of the pastry.

"I used to get into mischief when I was your age," Uncle Izzecha confided. "Perhaps it is being the youngest. You have to get attention somehow."

"Father doesn't give me attention either way," Runa said, picking flakes of pastry off her lap. "He's too busy."

"Well, he was worried about you last night. Had the palace turned upside down looking for you."

"How do you know?"

"I Sent to him last night to tell him you were with me."

Runa licked her fingers and wondered if it would be greedy to take another.

"How angry was he?" she asked.

"Relieved, not angry," Uncle Izzecha said. "Especially when he heard about the flesh traders."

"Did he mention Lelanta?"

Uncle Izzecha gave Runa a sympathetic grin.

"He did."

"Has he changed his mind?"

"I'm afraid not," Uncle Izzecha said, turning Runa's stomach into a stone. "In fact, he asked me if I would escort you there since I was planning to journey north myself in a day or two."

"Oh," Runa swallowed hard against the tears that suddenly burned in her eyes. Her throat ached. She was not even allowed home first. Father must be angrier than ever, despite what Uncle Izzecha had said. She crumpled slightly in her seat and Uncle Izzecha got up to move around his desk.

"Come, come," he said, lifting her head with his finger. "Is school so bad? I found it easier at school than at Lorandia. More friends to play with. I was one among

75

many, instead of being singled out as a prince."

"There are no dragons," Runa sighed deeply. "And I doubt the other girls would want to be friends with me. I don't seem to like the things most girls do."

"You cannot be the only girl to prefer dragons to dresses," Uncle Izzecha smiled kindly, and Runa wished King Mabrigas could understand her as Uncle Izzecha seemed to. Or at least that he would try.

"Now, if you are to travel with me and have at least a week without your possessions, we really ought to acquire an outfit or two for you. What do you say?"

"As long as they aren't pink," Runa said, fingering the fabric of her borrowed dress. Uncle Izzecha pleased her greatly with his loud laugh.

"No pink!" he agreed.

80 ✳ ෆ

The following morning Runa left Faradel in her uncle's caravan, excitement tickling her stomach. Uncle Izzecha had business in the port of Afrada first and so they were travelling east across the mountains before sailing around the northern point of Feldemoore for Lelanta on the far side. Knowing that such an adventure lay before her delaying her arrival at Lelanta, Runa felt she could enjoy herself. Her only disappointment was Uncle Izzecha's insistence that she travel to Afrada in a curtained litter, rather than on a pony.

"You are not used to long journeys," he said. "You will be sore and tired."

Runa had wanted to argue; in fact, had she been at home she would have protested and made everyone miserable until she got her way. But Uncle Izzecha had been so generous – he had bought her two dresses, both simply cut, undecorated, and hard-wearing as she had requested, instead of the usual delicate frippery that the Mistress Leira and the seamstress insisted were befitting for a princess. She was wearing the travelling dress today, a simple knee-length tunic of green over a darker green kirtle that fell almost to the floor. A russet-brown, rain-proof cloak was rolled and stowed in her bag in case the air turned cold. The leather belt was also brown with a design embossed in gold that reminded her of the artwork from Callenlas, where Elior was King. Her mother's paperknife was buckled to her hip, and her uncle had even given her a purse with a little silver to spend when they reached Lelanta. He had also purchased a pair of boys' boots for Runa, something she had always coveted but had never been allowed. They were comfortable and tough, of good-quality leather. She pulled her dress up so to admire them as the litter rocked along the road out of Faradel, born by two gigantic male servers.

Although she resented the litter, it gave Runa plenty of time to think and consider her uncle's words. Perhaps Lelanta would not be quite as bad as she thought. True, there were no dragons, but if she could manage, somehow, to behave herself for a year then perhaps father would allow her back to Lorandia. And perhaps, just perhaps, there might be another girl who felt the same as Runa about hairdressing and ruffles.

But the excitement of travelling quickly wore off. The day dragged on; the mountainous countryside passing slowly through the hazy fabric that enclosed Runa. Again, she wished she had been permitted a pony, for reading made her feel sick with the swaying of the litter. She felt restless and irritable when at last they reached the hunting lodge where they were to spend the night. Uncle Izzecha helped Runa out of the litter. As they stood about in the yard, a large blue patrol dragon swooped overhead, its wings stirring the straw strewn over the cobbles.

Runa's heart pounded. She wanted to watch the dragon soar out of sight but Uncle Izzecha hurried her inside.

It took them another day to reach Afrada. As they descended the last hill, the ocean came into view, glittering under the bright evening light of the Day-Star in summer. Runa sat up in the litter and peeked around the curtains at the front. It was so beautiful, so vast. She had only been to the coast twice in her life and each time the sea and sky caught her up in wonder at their enormity and beauty. She loved the mountains and would hate to live somewhere flat, but the sea with its endless expanse and potential to carry you to unknown lands and places filled her with a similar longing to the dragons.

Afrada, Feldemoore's southernmost port, nestled in a cove between the lower reaches of two hills. Three long piers stretched out into the sparkling water and the quayside was always bustling with traders, sailors, and King Mabrigas's harbourmasters. Several ships lay in the harbour, knocking gently against the wooden quays as the waves shifted them against their moorings.

Runa was surprised when Uncle Izzecha led them to a small house right by the water; she had expected to stay in the city governor's mansion.

"I thought you might prefer privacy," he said, when Runa asked him later that evening, over a game of Castles. Her heart warmed to him even further.

"Will you stay a few days?" she asked, moving one of her tokens.

"Stay?"

"When we get to Lelanta. Please. Stay a few days, just until I'm settled in?"

"Oh, Lelanta. Yes, of course."

Uncle Izzecha suddenly seemed distracted. Not concentrating, he lost the game and sent Runa up to her room for bed early.

"We have an early start in the morning," he said.

⁝ ✳ ℭ

Uncle Izzecha had not lied. A bleary-eyed maid woke Runa when the moon was still up, glancing off the water with a delicate, milky light. Runa dressed while half-asleep, declining breakfast, and was ushered out of the house with her cloak wrapped tightly about her.

Uncle Izzecha was already aboard the ship he had commissioned, a medium-sized galley with a hold full of Taranatian silk destined for Meretheos in the west.

"Get below for now," he told Runa, delighting her with such nautical language. "The sailors won't want you underfoot while we are leaving port."

Runa obeyed, too enchanted to refuse, for the ship was swaying gently beneath her feet and the ocean lay under the stars, waiting for them. They would not reach Lelanta for another three days. Three days of being a sailor, swabbing decks and hoisting sails.

A tiny cabin, barely a cupboard, had been set aside for her. Runa spent all of five minutes stowing her possessions carefully in the very pleasing little nook that had been built under her bunk. She had a tiny area of floor in which to dress and wash, and a single, tiny window. She pressed her face against the thick glass and watched as Afrada grew smaller and smaller, its lights going out one by one as the Day-Star rose and the sky lightened.

By the time the port would have been fully awake it was out of sight, and the waves were big enough to make walking difficult. Runa practised keeping her footing but it was difficult in such a tiny room, so she dared to venture out on deck.

The single mast bore a white, square sail, now fully unfurled to catch the wind which was driving them rapidly offshore. The deck stretched before Runa, its boards smooth and scrubbed, bleached by the Day-Star and salt water. Runa leaned over the rail, watching the sides of the boat slice through the water, sending white ripples away in angled lines.

Uncle Izzecha was nowhere to be seen so Runa found a couple of sailors mending nets who were willing to talk to her and plied them for information on everything from how to catch a fish to how to climb the rigging without falling into the sea. She learned as much sailor vocabulary as she could, intending to impress her uncle later with her knowledge.

At noon, Runa was called to join Uncle Izzecha for

lunch in the captain's cabin. To her surprise there was someone else present, a rolling, fat man swathed in coral silk and wearing a very orange turban. His fingers glittered with bright jewels, and a large emerald quivered at the centre of his turban with every move he made. He reminded Runa of the jesters and acrobats who entertained her father's court on special occasions, except that their jewels were made of glass while his were undoubtedly real. The idea of the oversized stranger attempting a somersault made Runa snort with laughter. She pretended to smother a sneeze while she regained her composure.

"Runa," Uncle Izzecha cast her a warning glance – Runa was sure he had seen through her poor cover. "I would like to present to you Lord Swarlor of Tyresis."

"Isn't that in tSardia?" Runa asked lightly, taking her seat at the table.

"Well, you have been paying attention in your lessons," Lord Swarlor complimented her, offering a plate of stuffed dates.

"Not really," Runa said honestly. "Some stuff sticks. I don't get to decide what."

Lord Swarlor chuckled. When he spoke, it was in the staccato accent of the south, his s's slightly slurred.

"My city is very near our border with Callenlas. We have often wished to be across the border."

"Lord Swarlor is a trader," Uncle Izzecha explained. Runa, busy filling her plate, did not much care, but tried to look as though she were listening. "He wishes to oversee the sale of his silks in Meretheos."

Runa nodded politely. She had hoped to have a cosy meal with her uncle and quiz him on his voyages and ambassadorial missions (she was certain he had been as far as Taranata, if not further afield). But now that it seemed Uncle Izzecha would be discussing business with Lord Swarlor all Runa wished to do was eat and get back out on deck.

Lord Swarlor questioned her courteously about her studies and her interests and Runa tried to give sensible answers that would not disgrace her father. Eventually she escaped back on deck and found a sailor to teach her the different types of knot used on board the ship.

By the following day, Runa felt that she was a worthy seafarer. She had learned to swagger, rather than walk, and so keep her balance on the shifting deck. She helped secure the sail when the captain ordered it fully unfurled, and the sailors admired her knots and told her she was a good apprentice. The captain was a kind man with a greying beard and thirty years' experience of both the sea and children, and he allowed Runa a brief turn at the helm.

But his eyes watched the horizon carefully. He

frowned as the sail billowed full one minute, then hung slack and void the next.

"A storm's brewing," he said, more to himself than Runa. "Can I trust you with the tiller a moment, while I speak with your uncle?"

"Of course!" Runa grinned and pretended that the captain did not afterwards ask his first mate to stand at her elbow and steady her hand.

Runa had her eye on the crow's nest as her next point of exploration, but her gaze was drawn by the captain and Uncle Izzecha. They were standing just below her, on the deck outside Uncle Izzecha's cabin. Runa could not hear their words, but both were gesturing avidly. Uncle Izzecha's usually calm face was flushed and tight. Runa felt uncomfortable and curious.

The captain returned and smiled distractedly at Runa.

"I must take the tiller now," he said. "I want to draw nearer the shore and weigh anchor until the storm is past."

"Is that why you were arguing with Uncle Izzecha?" Runa asked.

The captain gave her a sharp look.

"Yes," he said, guardedly. "Your uncle feels we should press on. But I will not jeopardise the safety of my men. Not for any deadline.

"Now, you take the advice of an old man, my Lady.

84

Curiosity is good to a point. But it'll get you into no end of trouble. Don't meddle in things you aren't meant to know."

"I won't," Runa said with a bright smile. She had learned to comply with adults' instructions, outwardly at least. Arguing just brought trouble.

But of course, she had no intention of not meddling. Something was afoot and her suspicions lay with Lord Swarlor. What was a tSardian Lord doing aboard a Feldemoorian ship, travelling north? Not selling silks, Runa was certain. And Uncle Izzecha's anxiety about pausing in their journey seemed strange also; was he at Lord Swarlor's mercy? Threatened with death or disgrace?

Runa scrambled down the ladder onto the deck, wondering where to begin. Lord Swarlor's cabin was in the bows – the front – of the ship, so that was as good a place as any. Perhaps she could search it? But as she drew nearer, looking as innocent as she could, she could hear snores rumbling from inside the cabin. She peaked through the small window and could see the vast, coral pink form of Lord Swarlor spilling over the sides of his bunk, his mouth gaping open, his jewelled hand trailing on the floor.

Listening, Runa had learned, was the best way to understand what was going on in the grown-ups' world.

Grown-ups would never voluntarily tell you anything. But through listening at keyholes and behind curtains, Runa had learned most of what was going on at the palace. Most of it was boring, admittedly, but every so often, she had discovered something important. Lord Swarlor was certain to wake soon, and then she could spy on him through the window and listen to his conversations. She would learn what he was up to.

Runa sank down onto the narrow strip of deck that ran between Lord Swarlor's window and the rail of the ship. She leaned against the wall of the cabin and watched the sea. One of the sailors had told her of giant fish that spouted great jets of water, and Runa was determined to see one if it came near the ship.

But the Day-Star beat warmly on the deck and the swaying of the ship was soothing, and Runa slipped into sleep.

CHAPTER 9

Lord Lur's presence shot through Zaphreth's mind like a bolt of lightning. He sat up with a gasp of either pain or shock, it was hard to tell, and scattered sand left and right as he searched for the General.

The desert lay about him, the fire mere embers, Wirrat's snoring form a humped shadow against a thorn bush.

Zaphreth drew a shuddering breath. It had been a dream. Or else the General had been searching for him. His power of mind was so great he could easily See this far. Most could only Send messages a short distance; a few across a city. Lord Lur's power was palpable; the two times Zaphreth had met him, the air around him had seemed to vibrate with dominion.

The first time had been that afternoon at the barracks, after the fight with Eldor. Master Filias had led him along a dimly lit hallway, giving Zaphreth the uneasy sense that he should not be here. There was a smell of dust and ancient stone and a trace of the catacombs built beneath to house the rich and important dead.

A single door stood at the end of the corridor, cut of a dark stone, with a large star carved in relief over the entire surface. Zaphreth wondered that there was no guard, though the atmosphere in the corridor was forbidding enough. Although the corridor was built of the same polished stone as the rest of the palace, the sound of Zaphreth's feet was dull and repressed, as though the air itself was heavy with the General's presence.

The door opened silently to Master Filias's knock, and Zaphreth stepped cautiously inside.

A long, low hall stretched before him, built entirely of black polished stone. Lamps stood in alcoves along the wall, but the stone caught the light and seemed to trap it within its depths, dulling its glow. The ceiling was the height of two men, but because the hall was so long and wide it felt oppressively low.

Two guards stepped out from either side of Zaphreth, pointing their glinting spears at his throat. Zaphreth stood dead still.

At the end of the hall, on a throne of the gleaming black stone, elevated on a dais edged with gold, sat a male figure. He wore black trousers and a tunic of white silk, with a sleeveless robe of vermilion satin falling to the floor. The robe had a high collar which stood up around his ears, and the entire thing was edged in stiff gold embroidery, glittering with small jewels. On his head sat a circlet of gold, set with rubies. One of his legs was bent, the ankle resting on his other knee, in an attitude casual of the power at his fingertips.

As Zaphreth looked at the figure he felt a knee-weakening force probing through his mind, like a piercing beam of light searing into his soul, searching his deepest being. It did to Zaphreth's soul what the full strength of the Day-Star might have done to his eyes, had he looked.

Zaphreth staggered, fighting the dizziness which threatened to overcome him. At last, his mind was released, and he was able to open his eyes. But he felt raked within, stripped naked and vulnerable. He had to resist the desire to cover himself with his hands as he opened his eyes and discovered that he was still clothed, still standing between the spears of the guards.

"Zaphreth, son of Irek, of the village of Havara."

It was not a question. Zaphreth bent his head in a bow of acknowledgement.

The General stood, flicking the length of his robe behind him, stepping down off the dais to pace slowly towards Zaphreth. Zaphreth licked his lips.

A gesture from the General removed the spears from Zaphreth's throat and the guards stood back to attention.

"Welcome to my hall, Zaphreth," the General said. Now that he was closer, Zaphreth could see his smooth skin, his neatly trimmed and combed beard, and the impeccable cut of the hair. There was a scent of expensive oil, mingled with cloves and lime. But Zaphreth could not help feeling it was masking something else, a tinge of unpleasantness, like meat left out for too long.

The General smiled at Zaphreth, his teeth were white and straight. The weight of his attention was all but unbearable, but Zaphreth tried to square his shoulders and take it. This was everything he had ever wanted, to be recognised by the great and powerful in the world. He must not fail now.

Master Filias approached the General with several small, quick bows. The General inclined his ear with a trace of impatience to the man, who now seemed fussy and old with his silly little tasselled hat, beside the magnificent form of the General. Master Filias whispered into the General's ear, who kept his attention on Zaphreth, before straightening and considering Zaphreth with renewed interest.

"So Master Filias seems to think that your skill in Mind Powers is exceptional."

"I suppose ..."

"I dislike modesty, boy."

Zaphreth drew a breath and tried again.

"Yes, Lord. I am skilled in Mind Powers."

"Not many can bear my inner eye upon them and remain standing," the General said. Zaphreth's fingers tingled as he remembered that sense of being raked through and through when he first entered the room.

"Have you had any training in Mind Powers?"

"No training, Lord," Zaphreth answered. "My parents taught me to light fires and make light. Nothing more."

"Mm. I am driving my Masters to push the use of Mind Powers as far as they can. Magic too. There are things we can accomplish beyond anyone's imaginings. Progress. That is what we want."

Zaphreth remained silent. He knew nothing of these things. He knew daily hunger and begging, and fathers marching away to prison and death. He knew shame and disgrace and wanted that to end. If Mind Powers and magic would help bring victory to his country and honour to himself then he would use them.

"We are looking for young men like you with a natural capacity for the power of the mind."

Zaphreth stood a little taller at being called a man.

"I would be willing to train in anything, Lord."

The General seemed pleased with the answer. Zaphreth took a risk and spoke on.

"We have endured war long enough. I wish to bring justice and peace to my people."

91

"Justice," the General's dark eyes flashed with an inner fire until they glowed red, but his mouth smirked as though Zaphreth had told a dirty joke. "Justice. Yes."

The General placed a confidential arm about Zaphreth's shoulders. Had the proximity of the great leader not made Zaphreth's legs tremble, he would have enjoyed the moment more.

"Master Filias here has been doing some research into your family," the General spoke in a low voice, so that only Zaphreth could hear.

"My family?" he queried.

Master Filias had drawn back a little, and the General was leading Zaphreth up the hall to the dais. Zaphreth fought his inner trembling, determined to make the most of this opportunity. A stray thought wished Eldor and the other boys were here to see him now, the scruffy apprentice embraced by the General of tSardia.

"Well, we were curious as to where your exceptional skill in Mind Powers came from," the General spoke in his smooth, conspiratorial voice. "Usually, such capacity is only found in the ruling classes, you understand."

Zaphreth did not, but nodded, not wishing to appear foolish.

"We understand from palace records that your mother served in Prince Lakesh's court here in Sarreia for quite a number of years."

Zaphreth frowned.

"She was in the household of ..." the General snapped his fingers at Master Filias, who scurried forward. "The boy's mother," the General muttered in irritation. "Her name, her house?"

"Rusi of Havara, my Lord; she served Prince Herodas."

"Exactly, Prince Herodas, Lakesh's younger brother."

Zaphreth shook his head, his hair brushing the General's silk-clad forearm.

"I think there has been some mistake, Lord," he said, with a nervous laugh. "My mother is Ama of Havara."

"Daughter of Ishal?"

They stopped now at the dais, and the General turned Zaphreth to look into his face. Zaphreth's heart was racing; he could not comprehend what the General was getting at. He felt foolish and curled his toes inwards, desperate to appear competent and above all, useful.

"Yes, Lord. Ishal was my grandfather. But it is a common name. Surely there could be several Ishal's of Havara ..."

The General's eye was fixed on Zaphreth, that strange, orange light flickering in its depths again.

"Rusi was Ama's younger sister," the General said. "She served in the household of Prince Herodas."

Zaphreth felt dizzy as he began to piece together the information the General was laying before him.

"Ama is not my mother?"

"It seems Rusi left the palace quite suddenly, and never returned. Our records suggest that she died about four months later, perhaps in childbirth?"

Zaphreth swallowed, and this time his legs buckled. The woman he thought was his mother, Ama, was actually his aunt. His real mother was ... dead.

"Here, sit." The General pushed him down onto the edge of the dais, snapping his fingers again at Master Filias. A fine glass was pushed into Zaphreth's hand and the General forced it to his lips. Fire filled Zaphreth's mouth and scorched his throat, but the shock brought some clarity to his mind. He slowly raised his eyes to the General, his heart pounding, his mouth dry. He heard himself pronounce the words with disbelief.

"My father is a prince? Prince Herodas?"

"It seems very likely ..." the General said, his mouth curled in amusement. "It would certainly explain the exceptional power you possess."

Zaphreth's head whirled with questions, but his heart beat out a song: this was why he was so discontent, why he felt so out of place as an apprentice, why he had felt so wrong all his life. He was the son of a prince, meant for a life of power and comfort.

"Where is my father now?" Zaphreth asked, still dazed.

"Sadly, he died, several years ago now. He fell from a

terrace in Essola."

"What happens now?" Zaphreth asked. He thought he should appear sad to hear that his real father had died, but the truth was he felt nothing. It was hard to feel sad for a man he had only just heard of.

"Well, there is little I can do for you immediately," the General said. "With the war the king has bigger concerns than to establish the rights of his younger brother's illegitimate son."

Zaphreth felt the small offence in the General's words, and flinched, but he nodded understanding.

"Perhaps you could enter my service for a while," the General suggested, examining the rings on his hand. "You could prove yourself useful, worthy of the nobility you were born to, and work towards the 'justice' you desire for your people."

Zaphreth nodded eagerly. This was what he had desired and more. To serve the General, to be part of his personal Guard, instead of just an ordinary soldier. And of course, once the war was over, he would be recognised. All he had wanted ultimately was a nice house in the city. Now, there would be palaces, gardens, servants ...

"I will serve you, my Lord," Zaphreth said, jumping to his feet to stand beside the General. Unfortunately, his sudden action sent a sluice of liquid slapping onto the stone at his feet. He reddened and set the glass down on the dais, before straightening his tunic.

"I require blood," the General said, narrowing his eyes.

Zaphreth swallowed.

"When you pledge to me, you pledge your life. You promise to serve me to the death."

"I will, my Lord," Zaphreth nodded eagerly. After all, with such a General, this war could not last very long at all.

"Very good," the General said. "From now on you will be admitted to my confidences. I will honour you by revealing my name to you. You must speak it only to those who know me. If you speak my name to another, I will know it and there will be consequences. My name is your badge; speak my name as a password to your brothers in my service."

Zaphreth hardly took any of this in; his mind was swirling with desires, ideas and thoughts. He was the son of a prince, and was to now be associated with the General.

"Kneel, Zaphreth of Havara," the General said.

Zaphreth knelt, the cold stone pressing painfully against his knees.

"Do you swear loyalty to me, as your General and Lord? Do you swear to keep the secret of my name and to serve me with all your strength, even to death? Do you offer me your life's blood as your pledge?"

"I do," Zaphreth said.

"Your knife?"

Fumbling, Zaphreth drew out his knife from his belt and held out the hilt. The General took it and turned it over in his hand, examining the blade. It was a cheap knife but well used and cared for, Zaphreth's eighth birthday gift from his father ... from Irek.

"Then I accept your blood," the General said. "Hold out your hand."

Zaphreth obeyed, feeling somewhat remote and empty. The General drew the knife across his palm; there was a moment of searing pain which Zaphreth fought so that he barely winced, and his blood dripped heavy onto the stone.

"My name is Lur," the great man whispered, holding out his palm to meet Zaphreth's. His nostrils flared at the smell of blood.

Then the knife was back in Zaphreth's hand, and he was being escorted through the door by the guards.

"Report to the barracks tomorrow morning," Lur called after him, before the heavy door was closed.

಄ ✳ ಞ

Even miles from Sarreia, and six months since that first encounter, the weight of the memory was oppressive.

The cool air of the desert night was hard to breathe. Zaphreth had still not fully worked out the emotions he experienced in Lord Lur's presence. There was certainly awe and admiration, but a strong sense of fear and anxiety also. There was the pleasure of speaking with one of the greatest men in Sarreia, possibly even the entire land, and having his attention and even pleasure ... yet with it a sense that he mattered nothing at all, and that as soon as the conversation was over, Lur would return to his usual work and not think about Zaphreth again.

Still, Zaphreth's admiration for the General was undiminished. Great men had to be ruthless, that was why they were great, surely. It was why Lord Lur was so successful as a warrior, as a leader in war; he was not troubled by details of men's lives. There was work to be done, and he did it.

And hadn't Zaphreth done the same thing? He had ignored Ama's disappointment and tears and forged ahead with what he knew to be right, wearing the black uniform of the General's Guard, attending his training in the barracks, and in Master Filias's study, perfecting his control of his Mind's Power.

Eldor's face, when Zaphreth passed him in the pillared training yard one day, had been worth every blister and aching muscle. Zaphreth had inclined his head in a gracious nod of recognition and it had taken all his powers of self-control to hide the glee that bubbled up in his chest, as Eldor's mouth hung open. His widened eyes had followed Zaphreth across the yard, in his black uniform.

Lying sleepless on the cold desert sand, Zaphreth could not help thinking that this was not quite what he had imagined serving Lord Lur would entail. He had envisioned glorious battle charges or important meetings with the officials of tSardia, not slogging across the desert with an irascible companion of questionable loyalty, sneaking into enemy territory.

Weary, Zaphreth sank into his favourite reverie, his life after the war, when his mission was complete. Lord Lur would speak to Prince Lakesh. There would be a ceremony, a recognition of his rights as the lost son of a prince of tSardia. Zaphreth wondered how many palaces he would be granted. Perhaps he could have one in tSama, with balconies overlooking the glittering ocean, and a pool on a leaf-shaded terrace. A whole room of clothes, silk tunics and those shimmering robes worn by the highest nobles in tSardia. People bowing and skittering after his every whim.

He had paid his dues, after all; he deserved it, after so many years of ignominy and shame.

CHAPTER 10

Even though Zaphreth had slept badly, it was Wirrat who woke grouchy and irritable. With a grunt, the guide told Zaphreth to pack up and set out.

Watching him carefully, Zaphreth felt about in the bottom of his pack. He could feel the scabbard of the small sword he had hidden among his clothes, the spare pair of sandals, but ... not the pouch.

Zaphreth's heart pounded and his ears grew hot. Where was it? The pouch of gold Lord Lur's servant had given him. It was to keep him once he got into Callenlas; Zaphreth had intended to use it to support his story, that he was the son of a tSardian noble, disillusioned with his country's politics and ambitions. Few would believe he was noble if he had no money.

Something clinked against his fingers as he rummaged in the bottom of the pack, trying not to betray his anxiety to Wirrat. Relief flooded Zaphreth as he felt the circular coins through the leather of the pouch. It was there.

Feeling guilty towards Wirrat (for his first suspicion had been that the guide had stolen the gold), Zaphreth hurried after his companion. Wirrat thrust a round of dry bread into Zaphreth's hand. Breakfast. As soon as they were off this accursed desert, Zaphreth intended to find an inn and treat himself and Wirrat to a meat pie and a cool ale. His mouth watered at the thought of it.

"How far until Hirath's Ridge?" Zaphreth asked, through a mouthful of the bread. He had been chewing it for a while now, but still could not swallow it. It moved around his mouth like a damp coagulation of sawdust.

"I reckon we'll reach it this evening," Wirrat said. The thought seemed to cheer him a little, but he continued, "if you can pick your feet up, that is."

Zaphreth pushed his lips together and chose not to respond.

෨ * ෬

As the day wore on, the dust at their feet became coarser, mingled with dirt. Patches of dry grass and low, thorny shrubs became more frequent. Wirrat shot a rabbit to supplement their meagre supplies of oats and oil. They cooked it over a fire and spent their last night in the desert, before climbing the final dune with the Day-Star in the morning.

Then they came to Hirath's Rift and stood at its edge, stunned by the view. The rift was a low cliff that cut north to south along the landscape. It marked the edge of the desert, giving way to farmlands that spread as far as the eastern sea. Zaphreth stared at an alien landscape, lush and full of colour even in the grey morning light.

The land ahead had been divided into fields, some yellow-green with ripening wheat, some leafy and lush, some striped with crops planted in rows. Orchards stood in bushy relief near farmhouses with peculiar sloping roofs. Raised in the ochre plains, Zaphreth felt like a man presented with a lake after only ever drinking from a well. He sank onto the cliff top and watched the Day-Star rise, tinting all the green with gold, drawing out new colours as it grew in strength until the whole world seemed to vibrate with beauty. It was almost too much to bear. Zaphreth had never imagined there could be so many shades of green, ranging from almost yellow in paleness to the deep, dark green of the forests to the north.

The forests. His destination.

Drawn from his admiration, Zaphreth shook himself lightly and got to his feet. He could not stay here. He had to make progress.

"Finished your daydream?" Wirrat asked, wryly.

Zaphreth allowed himself to imagine giving Wirrat a gentle shove with his mind as he strode towards the edge of the Rift. He felt the pleasure of the look of surprise on Wirrat's creased face as he fell, his mouth open in a shocked 'O'.

Then Zaphreth imagined trying to find the border crossing alone, and navigating the unknown land below, and restrained himself.

Wirrat led him along the cliff edge until he found one of the narrow paths that zig-zagged down the cliff. Hirath's Rift was not especially high, perhaps the height of a house of four storeys, but the path was steep and at times little more than a track in the sandy dirt. It would be too easy to slip and fall, perhaps not to death, but certainly to a miserable fracturing of bones and the ruin of the rest of one's life.

Zaphreth picked his steps carefully, and even the brash Wirrat did the same.

"We'll head north now," Wirrat said, nodding his head at the farmlands to their left. "The forests aren't far as the crow flies, but the roads wind around fields and villages, so it'll take us a day."

After slogging through the desert, the stony road at their feet made their pace feel fast, and the air was still cool and fresh. It was high summer and the fields they passed on either side of the road were overflowing with produce. Zaphreth saw long stretches of yellowing grain and barley; smaller, cottage gardens with neat rows of juicy radishes and watermelons; and orchards, their fruit yet to swell, but ripening fast into globes of sweetness.

Perhaps this was where he would live, he thought. He could buy some of these fields, hire men to work them, build a fine house next to a vineyard. It felt so fresh and green.

As the day wore on, however, the heat increased. It was not as burning as the desert, but the air felt humid and thick. Zaphreth sweated in his tunic and Wirrat wiped his brow often. They stopped to drink from a stream and share the leftovers of last night's rabbit.

"It'll probably storm tonight," Wirrat commented, and that was all he said during the entire rest.

As evening drew on, Zaphreth could see the forest again, dark green and leafy, across the last field. A village was built in the shadow of the forest and Wirrat strode in with confidence, though Zaphreth noticed a shift in his demeanour. He took more glances to his left and right and checked over his shoulder more than once.

The small market square was still busy, though most stalls and shops were closing up for the night. Wirrat pulled Zaphreth back and they watched the scene from the corner of a single-storey workshop.

"I don't like this," Wirrat said, in a whisper.

"What?" Zaphreth asked. He could see nothing out of the ordinary: a handful of women perusing the stalls before they closed, shop owners sharing gossip as they packed up their wares, folding coloured fabric and boxing up oranges and figs.

Wirrat nodded in the direction of an official looking building at the far end of the market square. A full guard of four men stood to full attention, wearing the dark blue cloaks of the king's army.

"They weren't here last time," he said darkly.

"So?" Zaphreth asked, with more irritation than was wise, but he was tired and hungry, and eager for this journey to be over.

"So," Wirrat explained, as if to a very young child. "If a guard has been posted in this town, with the border crossing just beyond in those trees there, I'd guess the Callenlasians are now paying more attention to the border. They probably have their own soldiers posted on the road."

Sulkily, Zaphreth acknowledged that this was a valid concern.

"We'll go around the back of the square and take a careful look ahead," Wirrat said.

Zaphreth sighed. He had been looking forward to his pasty and ale and a night in a soft bed before crossing the border in the early hours. He had also been looking forward to shaking Wirrat off at last.

Backing away from the busy square, Wirrat led Zaphreth round the back of the shops and houses, down a narrow, dirty alley, and out onto the other side. Here, Wirrat hesitated. An open field with a few grazing goats ran up to the forest. About a hundred and fifty paces away the road emerged from the town, leading into the forest.

"It's too open," Wirrat said, disappointed. "We'll have to risk going into the town tonight, stay in the tavern. I'll ask a few careful questions, find out our chances of getting over the border. Just tell people we're passing through."

ജ ✳ ഗ

Easing himself back against the wall of the tavern, Zaphreth sighed with contentment. He had just finished the best meal he had had for many years. The tavern was dark and not especially clean, and the bar was tended by a gum-mouthed old woman with dirty fingernails. But the skill of the cook accounted for the overflowing tables. The pie Zaphreth had ordered had been clattered down before him, a thick, crisp crust rising in a small mountain from a pewter dish, and when Zaphreth cut it open, the thick gravy dribbled over and pooled on the plate.

Zaphreth enjoyed every salty mouthful and ate until his stomach hurt.

Sitting back, his hands resting on either side of his distended belly, Zaphreth looked over to where Wirrat was hunched over a game of Hazard. The heap of coin in the centre of the table accounted for the intensity of the men around the table, but Wirrat had been ordering rounds with dangerous frequency for a man intent on winning. All he had eaten was a small pasty, gulping mouthfuls between the tossing of the counters. Zaphreth had to admire his capacity for drink, if nothing else. In his satisfied state, Zaphreth could even feel a vague, grudging fondness for the man, simply from spending so many hours together over the past eight days. Who knows, he thought, perhaps he would even miss having Wirrat's grumpy face across the fire each morning when he was alone in enemy territory.

CHAPTER 11

Wirrat shook Zaphreth awake when the light in the upper room of the tavern was still grey and pale. Zaphreth had almost refused to sleep there when Wirrat led him up, still walking and talking straight after a night of drinking. Ten mattresses lined the walls, covered in grey, woollen blankets, half of them already filled with the snores of drunken men.

One day, I'll sleep on a feather bed with satin sheets, Zaphreth reminded himself, swallowing his pride. In spite of the snoring, he fell asleep quickly, exhausted and with a full stomach.

"We leave now," Wirrat said.

Zaphreth grabbed his pack sleepily and followed his guide down the stairs.

"Soon, the farmers will be crossing the border with their carts. They take produce to the town of Ubereth over the border where the army pay better prices for it."

"Traitors," Zaphreth muttered.

"Don't be soft," Wirrat rebuked him scornfully. "They get more money to pay in taxes to King Lakesh, to fund his army."

Zaphreth did not quite see it in the same way but held his tongue. Soon none of this would matter.

"Anyway, you're going to go with them. Here." Wirrat thrust a pale tunic into Zaphreth's hands.

"What's this?" Zaphreth asked.

"Your disguise. No apprentices cross the border, only farm folk. Stick it on and get among the carts. No one'll notice you then."

Sceptical, Zaphreth took the tunic and ducked into the outhouse of the tavern. In the semi-darkness he pulled off his own, familiar tunic and replaced it with the one Wirrat had stolen for him. It felt strange, the fabric was softer than Zaphreth's usual clothes and the tunic fell almost to the floor. Only as he emerged from the outhouse did Zaphreth realise what Wirrat had given him to wear. It was a dress.

80 * 08

Thunder rumbled threateningly in the south, and large, purple clouds kept the morning darker than usual. A collection of carts were gathered in the market square, and more were rattling in from the various farms near the town. The soldiers Wirrat and Zaphreth had seen guarding the official buildings had been joined by others, and they wandered between the carts, lifting the canvas covers to check the contents, asking questions of the different farmers.

Most of the farmers were alone, but a few had servants or family with them. Not many children, but that, apparently, was why Zaphreth had to be dressed as a girl.

"The soldiers will be less suspicious of a girl, less likely to go asking questions and checking where you're from. Just keep your head down, walk near one of the carts, and if they ask you a question, pretend you're mute."

At this point Wirrat handed Zaphreth a bonnet, the kind with a peaked hood that girls wore when they worked in the fields. It shielded their faces from the noon light, but also from curious soldiers. Still, Zaphreth stared at Wirrat, wondering whether this was a deliberate ploy to humiliate him.

"No time," Wirrat said urgently. "Look – they're moving!"

Zaphreth followed the guide's finger to the carts at the front, which were creaking slowly onto the road, ready to cross the border into Callenlas.

"Thanks," Zaphreth said, awkwardly, wondering if he ought to pay Wirrat or offer him his palm.

"Go!" Wirrat urged, turning Zaphreth towards the square and shoving him. Zaphreth clamped on the bonnet, tying the strings under his chin, and shifted his pack higher.

He glanced uncertainly back at Wirrat but the strange man was already gone, slinking back into the alleyway before the rain came.

The storm was building; the air crackled in the south, the wind whipped the canvas covers on the carts and flicked at the sides of Zaphreth's bonnet. He ducked his head down and tried to keep close to a cart like Wirrat had said, without attracting the notice of either the farmers or the soldiers. The farmers ignored him – none of them wanted trouble – and Zaphreth began to think that Wirrat had, annoyingly, been right.

The road into the forest, which yesterday had seemed so short, now seemed to stretch on forever. The carts creaked along it at a snail's pace, the soldiers marching ahead and behind. Zaphreth's heart was in his mouth the whole time, but they continued without incident. If anyone had been looking closely at him, they would have seen that he did not walk a bit like a shy farm girl, but everyone's attention was on the storm, and on crossing the border without trouble.

The first spots of rain began to smack the road as they drew near to the trees. The soldiers were in a hurry, nodding uneasy greetings to the Callenlasian guard who stood on the other side of the trees. The carts were waved through in haste, for the rain was becoming heavier by the minute, the wind dragging at the trees so that their leafy limbs rolled like waves of the sea.

At last, they passed the soldiers, and the farmers urged their horses to a faster pace. Zaphreth had to jog to keep up with the caravan as it wound deeper into the forest, wooden wheels rattling over the uneven road, the dust rapidly turning to a slippery mud. The trees grew thickly, but even here the rain hammered through; it was so heavy. The thunder grumbled, shaking the road beneath them. Lightning flashed overhead, shooting purple fingers across the menacing clouds.

At a fork in the road, the carts turned east, following the broader path to Ubereth. Zaphreth went with them a little way to avoid suspicion, but as soon as he could he slipped into the trees and turned back the way they had come. The other path went north, but soon bent around to head westward.

His relief at crossing the border made him walk lightly for a while, but soon the trees thinned out and the rain fell like water from a bucket, drenching Zaphreth through. He had never experienced such rain – what little fell in Sarreia was heavy, but brief. This rain continued unabated for hours, sometimes easing so that he thought it would pass, but then falling harder than ever. The wind drove the rain about in gusts and pushed Zaphreth back and forth along the path. The thunder shook the ground, the lightning creased the sky and, once, hit just a stone's throw away from him, splitting a tree with a vicious cracking sound. Fire flickered in the dry interior of the tree but was quickly extinguished.

Zaphreth became very afraid but had no idea what he should do. He wanted a cave or a house, or anything to take shelter in, but the forest continued unbroken whichever way he looked.

The clouds now completely covered the Day-Star, and Zaphreth lost all sense of direction. The oppressive heat had lessened, in fact, now a chill set into his body, the wet clothes sticking to his skin, the wind pressing into him to freeze his fingers, and even his bones.

He staggered on, cursing the weather, cursing King Elior, cursing his lot of birth which had led him to this.

The darkness grew thicker and Zaphreth guessed it was evening. The thunder and lightning had continued northwards, but the rain still fell. Exhausted and frozen, Zaphreth crawled under the spreading branches of an evergreen and found the pine needles damp, rather than sodden. He rummaged in his pack. Everything was wet and all he had to eat was soggy bread. He rummaged further and further again. Where was it?

Zaphreth dug, pulling out his tunic, his knife, his spare shoes, his blanket ... Where was the gold? He tipped the pack up, shaking it to eject anything that had escaped his numb fingers.

It was gone.

He had left his pack for that brief moment when he went to change his tunic. Such a fool he was!

And curse Wirrat. Curse the ground he walked on, the bed he slept in, the food he ate, curse every last minute of his miserable, selfish life!

Burning with rage, Zaphreth raised his hand, ready to throw out a blast of force that would destroy any trees in its path. But suddenly his arm dropped limply to his side. He was exhausted, and if he used up all his energy there would be nothing left for him to continue with in the morning. With no food and no money, he was left with nothing but his wits.

Zaphreth curled onto his side, miserable. He wanted to howl like a baby. He wanted, for a moment, to creep into Ama's arms and be comforted. But not only was he miles from home, he was also years beyond such behaviour.

He had never felt so desolate.

CHAPTER 12

Waking with a start, Runa looked about herself, trying to work out where she was. The Day-Star was setting, sinking into the sea behind her. The air was cold. All was still: the water, the ship, even the wind. It felt eerie. Runa got to her feet cautiously.

Leaning on the railing, she could see a strip of land in the distance. The captain had drawn nearer shore as he had wished. A long strip of pale beach led to a steep rise, growing thickly with forest. It was pleasing, after two days of nothing but sea and sky, to see something solid at last.

But something about the land was wrong. Runa frowned. It was something she felt should be obvious, but she couldn't think what.

Lord Swarlor! Remembering her suspicions, Runa whirled to peek inside the glass. The cabin was all in darkness and there was no sign of Lord Swarlor.

Should she search the cabin?

Runa snuck around to the door and tried it. It was locked.

"A storm is coming," Uncle Izzecha called across the deck from his cabin door, making Runa jump. "Better get below."

He pointed to the sky south of the setting Day-Star and Runa craned her neck to see over the cabins in the bows of the ship. Sure enough, the sky appeared bruised: purple and blue clouds gathered, tinged with an unhealthy yellow.

Runa nodded but as soon as her uncle was inside his cabin, she darted across the deck, for she had caught sight of Lord Swarlor's vivid robes behind her uncle. She crouched under the window which had been opened earlier when the day had been hot.

"This delay is most inconvenient," Lord Swarlor's southern accent marked his voice out.

"It will only hold us up by a few hours," Uncle Izzecha replied impatiently. "As soon as the storm is past, the captain will set sail again. We will be in Tyresis within two days, just a little later than planned."

"Lord Lur will not be pleased."

"Lord Lur should be pleased," Uncle Izzecha answered sharply. "We have in our hands a weapon that could turn the whole war in our favour. There is no way my brother will use force against us now."

Runa's heart was pounding, her thoughts darkening even as the clouds raced towards them overhead. A gust of wind suddenly pushed against her, lifting her hair and pressing her against the outer wall of her uncle's cabin. Her mind was a whirl, and she felt dizzy.

What was she to do? Could her uncle truly be plotting against her father? Tyresis was one of the tSardian ports – but who was Lord Lur?

And, of course, the land was on the wrong side of the ship. That was what was bothering her! If they were travelling north, the land would lie to port, but it did not. It stood to the right of the ship. They were heading south.

She had been right! Lord Swarlor was no silk trader. But her uncle ... Runa swallowed hard against the nausea of betrayal. She curled her hands into tight fists, forcing herself to stay calm and think clearly. She had wanted this adventure. She had wanted to prove that she could be a sky rider in her father's realm. But now she had a new, real opportunity – and more than that: here was an opportunity to serve the great King Elior of Callenlas.

Runa had caught rumours of this war that had been building for a number of years. tSardia had always wanted control of Callenlas; they saw it as their right and had been attacking the southern border relentlessly for years. They had recently mounted a greater attack, and it would make sense for Callenlas to seek the support of both northern kingdoms, Feldemoore and Meretheos, and even realms further afield, to defeat the tSardians once and for all.

Father had always been friendly with King Elior. Feldemoore and Callenlas were long allies; of course, the tSardians would want to keep them from joining forces in the war. What could they be threatening him with? Decimation by a powerful weapon? The first thing surely, was to find the weapon. Whatever it was it must be unthinkably powerful if it was enough to stop her father from joining forces against tSardia.

The obvious place to look seemed to be the hold. Runa slipped down the hatch into the dark belly of the ship. The galley was at the stern, the cargo in the bow – Runa threw open the door and found a stack of large wooden crates. None seemed large enough to hold a devastating weapon, but she was no master of war. She wanted to fight from the air, on the back of a silvery blue mountain dragon.

The crates were nailed down, but Runa found a crowbar and forced one open. Canvas protected its contents from water damage but when pushed aside Runa's hands came away filled with clouds of fine, violet silk. The next three crates were the same.

Runa ran her hands through her hair. The storm was almost upon them, the wind gusting hard now, the ship's flanks creaking and groaning.

Perhaps she should tell the captain. He had been kind to her and seemed a wise man. Runa made her way back up on deck, though her doubts began to rise as she went. If her uncle was a traitor – kind Uncle Izzecha – then who could she trust? What if the captain were in on the whole thing?

Uncle Izzecha was leaving his cabin as Runa's head emerged.

"I thought I told you to stay below!" he snapped. Runa ducked back down but peeped up to watch her uncle make his way up to the tiller to address the captain. While his back was turned, Runa scrambled across the deck and dived in through his door which he had left swinging open on its hinges.

Lord Swarlor had gone. The cabin was empty. What she expected to find, Runa had no idea, but she began searching frantically. Her uncle could return any moment. What she would do once she found the weapon she did not know either, but at least she would know what it was and where. Perhaps when they reached shore she could escape. But she would be miles from home and quite possibly in tSardia, surrounded by enemies.

Fat drops of rain began to spatter the glass and the

deck outside. The sky was dark now. Runa lit the lamp with a shaking hand, her mind's light wobbly and thin.

She started with the large desk, throwing open the top two drawers. She fell back in shock at the contents – vials and jars and boxes of magical ingredients: crushed lapis lazuli, dragon's blood, embers of a hangman's tree, and ground dragons' teeth, all labelled in her uncle's neat handwriting. In a lower drawer she found a box of spindly black twigs and a twisted wand.

The middle drawer was locked. Runa attempted to pick it (a skill she had learned two years before from one of the spit boys, who used to be a pickpocket). The lock glowed violet and sent a shock of heat through her fingers.

Runa stepped back and bumped into a small table. The ship was beginning to tilt now, her timbers creaking as the waters rose and moved her this way and that. The storm was building.

Something on the table had been unbalanced by Runa and helped by the movement of the ship it rocked and fell, cracking against the floor and rolling.

It was a seeing stone, the colour of blood with black shadows coiling through it.

Runa cried out in alarm. Her uncle was a magician, a sorcerer!

Her mind was working quickly. Perhaps, she thought,

the weapon uncle had in mind was magical. Surely that would make more sense than transporting a heavy weapon south on a small galley ship. Yes of course, he must have all the ingredients ready to form a powerful weapon that would convince her father, King Mabrigas, to remain out of the war. It must be enough to decimate large parts of Feldemoore, perhaps from a great distance.

With a cry of rage, Runa lifted the seeing stone and hurled it out of the open window. It landed with a satisfying splash in the churning sea. Heedless of what her uncle would do if he caught her, Runa snatched up handfuls of the magical ingredients and thrust them out of the window into the storm. Some smashed on the deck below, spilling bubbling acid or colourful potions out onto the wood. Runa cared not. All her thought was to destroy as many of the magical ingredients as possible and prevent her uncle from making whatever weapon he had planned.

The drawers were emptied quickly, but there was a cabinet also. It was curiously worked in a pearlescent lacquer, with many little doors and drawers. These ingredients were darker still, some burning Runa's hands as she carried them to the window, some sending a throbbing energy up her arms to her elbows. She was frightened, breathing heavily, inwardly as turbulent as the sea outside. For how could Uncle Izzecha be a traitor and a sorcerer? It was like a horrible dream.

The storm was almost overhead now, loud thunder cracking and the rain beating against the cabin. A flash of lightning filled the cabin with light, and there stood Uncle Izzecha, framed by the doorway, surrounded by wind and rain.

Runa froze for a moment, then pulled out another drawer and emptied it out of the window.

"What do you think you are doing?" Uncle Izzecha asked in a cold, stern voice. "These are magical ingredients. Some of them are very expensive. Some of them dangerous."

Runa stared at him, truly frightened now, but determined to take her stand against the enemies of King Elior, and her own people.

"I heard you," she cried, her voice catching on a sob as she thought of how her uncle had deceived her. "I heard you and the tSardian rebel! Traitor!"

She snatched up another box and threw it out.

Uncle Izzecha's eyes narrowed. He stepped towards her slamming shut the doors of the cabinet so that Runa could not take any more of its contents. He stood over her now, tall and forbidding in his dark robe. His eyes glittered with cool anger, and Runa thought that was more frightening than if he had blustered or even hit her.

"I threw it all away," she whispered. "So now you can't

make your weapon. Your plan is foiled. And I don't care what you do to me."

She did care, very much in fact, but a sky rider would never show such cowardice.

Uncle Izzecha was watching her carefully, and now a small sneer crossed his face.

"Do you think I would leave such a weapon just lying around my cabin for anyone to take? For anyone to lay their dirty fingers on and just toss into the sea?"

Runa's heart sank.

"Oh no," Uncle Izzecha reached out his hand and took hold of her shoulder, pinching it tightly so that Runa winced. He whispered in her ear, "I keep my weapons close, so they are safe."

Just then, the ship keeled alarmingly, and the entire cabin tilted almost into the sea. Runa screamed – she couldn't help herself – as all the contents of the cabin were thrown towards them. She bumped her head and heard glass smashing, and then cold water spilled over her from the window, making her gasp.

Then the ship, somehow, righted herself, and they staggered to their feet, Uncle Izzecha still with a tight grip on Runa's tunic.

He dragged her to the door of the cabin and out onto the deck where all was shouting and alarm. Sailors ran here and there, throwing out ropes and pails of seawater.

Uncle Izzecha took Runa to a barrel and coiled a thick rope around them both. He secured it tightly, binding them both to the barrel.

Runa was still dazed from hitting her head and could only cling on tightly as the ship lurched about, tossed by the furious sea. The mast came down, missing them narrowly, and then with a groan, the ship broke open.

Another wave tipped her entirely on one side, and Runa and her uncle were thrown into the water.

The cold brought Runa to her senses, but she only just managed to hold her breath. It was awful. The water churned and bubbled, and she clung to the barrel, her only solid contact in the whole whirling world. Twice she surfaced and managed to gasp a lungful of air before she was dragged under again, to be rolled over and over through bits of wood and snakes of rope.

At last, they were pulled away from the ship by the tide and managed to both be at the surface, clinging to the barrel and ropes. Runa stared across the barrel into her uncle's face and despised him. She wanted to hit him, scratch his face, but the sea was still throwing them back and forth, and there were too many bits of broken wood and cargo for Runa to take her eyes off the water. The lightning flickered, throwing into sharp relief the jagged waves and the sorry carcass of the ship slowly sinking beneath the surface. Runa could see other sailors flailing in the water, some gripping pieces of debris, some swimming for the shore.

Uncle Izzecha began to do the same, fighting the ocean and heading for the strip of darker shadow that indicated the beach. Runa felt it was sensible to work with him, though she checked her hip for her dagger and was relieved to find it there.

Then a rock grazed her leg, and she felt a shiver of fear.

"Uncle!" she spluttered. "There are rocks! Uncle!"

Then a wave sluiced over them both, and Runa was turning in the water. Something knocked her head. She saw stars and thought all was lost.

A large wave lifted Runa, the barrel, and Uncle Izzecha, dragging them in a terrifying rush to shore. Bruised and aching all over, feeling as though a nail was being hammered into her skull, Runa clung to the sand and fought to stay upright before the next wave broke over them.

She groaned and coughed up a great mouthful of salt water. Sitting up gingerly, she tried to get her bearings. She was near the northern end of a sandy beach where black, jagged rocks turned the waves white in places along the shallows. Some of the breakers rolling in were the size of a small house, thundering onto the shore. Perhaps a hundred paces inland lay a thick forest, the green crowding onto the beach, as if forest and sand were at war for the land.

The ship had keeled onto her side, dragged into the shallow water by the tide, and the waves were breaking around her. Runa could hear the groans of some of the sailors, and looking around there were some lying horribly still, among the rocks nearby.

Hampered by wet clothes and frozen fingers, Runa fumbled for her dagger and sawed through the thick ropes that still clung to her. Her breath came in great sobs, which she tried to suppress. Freed at last, she pulled herself closer to the barrel and peered cautiously around it.

An uneven shadow lay in the wet sand beyond the barrel. At first, Runa thought it was another rock, but then she saw pale fingers and knew it was Uncle Izzecha.

Runa stared sadly at him, betrayal as bitter as saltwater in her mouth. His face was pressed into the sand, an ugly gash still oozing blood across the side of his head. Runa's instincts were to run, to head for the trees and not stop until she had found safety.

But the freedom and safety of not one, but two nations, were at stake, not to mention her father's honour and King Elior's reign. What had Uncle Izzecha said? Runa's thoughts were fuzzy and her head throbbed, but she was impatient with herself.

"Think," she told herself sternly. She closed her eyes and drew a slow breath, taking herself back to the tilting cabin and her uncle's hissed words.

I keep my weapons close so that they are safe.

Close. What could be closer than on his own person?

With a great effort, Runa rolled her uncle onto his back and began searching his robes. There were many concealed pockets but nothing more inside them than a quill, a folded square of soggy parchment, and a bunch of keys.

Uncle Izzecha retched and brought up a mouthful of water. Runa startled and backed away, ready to run, but he only groaned and sank back into a daze. Then the starlight caught on something, dancing suddenly against a glassy surface among clothing.

Uncle Izzecha's pendant! The sapphire that had caught Runa's eye on their first meeting, ages ago now it seemed, in Faradel.

Runa grasped it and pulled it quickly over Uncle Izzecha's limp head. He groaned and his eyes rolled alarmingly.

Runa stood over him, the jewel tingling against her palm. It felt weighted, as though dense with magic, and she was unsure what to do with it. In the end, reluctantly, she slipped it around her own neck and between her sodden kirtle and tunic, unwilling to have it directly against her skin. If it was a weapon, King Elior and his advisors may need to examine it.

Now Runa fingered the hilt of her dagger, her mother's beautiful paper knife sharpened into a deadly weapon. If her uncle truly intended harm to Feldemoore and Callenlas, Runa knew she ought to do whatever she could to prevent it. Here he lay, unconscious and at her mercy.

Runa lifted the dagger, loosening it from its sheath, her heart thudding loudly in her ears.

The boat was gone. Her uncle's magic was all at the bottom of the sea. She had the weapon, or her best guess at it anyway. He was badly wounded, washed up on a beach, miles from anywhere. She hesitated.

Then Uncle Izzecha's hand gripped Runa's ankle.

She shrieked, kicking and writhing in the sand to escape his grip.

The dagger was in her fist and she stabbed his hand. With a yell and a curse, Izzecha let her go and Runa ran, harder than she had ever run before, for the trees. Her feet slipped in the soft sand; her wet skirts holding her back. Glancing behind her she could see Izzecha wrestling with the coils of rope that had saved his life. He cursed and raged, but Runa had the advantage.

She made it to the trees before he was free and crashed through the undergrowth in a panic. The trees and low shrubs were thick and close, ivy and thorns clinging at her like grasping fingers.

Stumbling on, Runa forced herself to keep going, though her head felt as though it would burst and all she wanted to do was curl up somewhere and sleep. Now that her initial shock was wearing off, the cold was creeping into her bones and she had to fight a foggy tiredness that threatened to pull her under.

"Keep going," she whispered hoarsely to herself, trying not to think of bats, or bears, or wolves. "Just keep going."

CHAPTER 13

"What do we have here, then?"

The voice that woke Zaphreth was coarse and slimy with greed. He could hear a clinking sound, and for a moment he thought he was back at home with Ama getting ready for the day. He felt stiff, hot and cold all at once, and there was a peculiar tingling sensation in his limbs and spine.

Zaphreth wanted to go back to sleep, but his throat burned. He sat slowly, looking for a drink.

He was not at home. His head brushed against rough branches as he sat and a shower of pine needles rattled down over him. The light scorched his eyes; its brightness told him it must be midday, or just past.

"Well, hello there, miss," the nasty voice said. Zaphreth blinked at the two shadows crouching nearby. They shifted and blurred, and he could not focus on them. His bag lay between them, its contents strewn across the ground.

His bag! Memory returned in a jumbled flash. Wirrat, the desert, the carts crossing the border ... his gold!

Zaphreth moved at last, trying to get up, reaching for his knife. But one of the men instantly aimed a long, evil-looking blade at his throat. Zaphreth froze, his limbs heavy and unwilling, his head spinning with the effort of staying upright.

"Interesting collection of things for a young maid to be carrying about in the forest," the man said, gesturing at Zaphreth's old tunic, the spare, fine one Lord Lur had given him, the collection of knives, and the various cooking implements Zaphreth carried. All were damp and crumpled.

"This is nice stuff," the other man grunted, holding the tunic to the light. "Worth a pretty penny."

"Now, how did a girl like you come by such a fine set of clothes?"

Why did they keep calling him a girl? Zaphreth's brain was sluggish. All he wanted to do was lie down and sleep.

"Up you get," the first man said, flicking the knife tip up to encourage obedience. Zaphreth shifted forward and managed, somehow, to force himself upright.

Only now did the man peer closer at him. He appeared to Zaphreth to be in a fog, his face rippling and clouded.

He seemed to have a moustache ... or did he have two mouths?

"Hang on," the man exclaimed. "It's a boy!"

There was amusement and a hint of anger in his voice, but the whole world began to hum, and the fog grew thicker. Then the forest floor rushed up at Zaphreth's face and he knew no more.

CHAPTER 14

Runa kept expecting to hear her uncle behind her, tearing at the branches and leaves, reaching for her arms, but she ran on in silence.

Eventually, lungs burning, her limbs like stone, she felt she could not take another step, and sank down against an ancient oak. Its rough bark gave her a sense of permanence and certainty in a world which now seemed as changeable as the sea. Runa pressed her hands over her face and drew a deep, shuddering breath.

So far, this adventure had not met any of her expectations. She was frozen, hungry, hurt and lost, and ... the realisation came to her with a thrill of horror: Her father thought she was safely on her way to Lelanta. No one would be looking for her for another day at least.

Tears poured down her cheeks, hot on her chilled skin. For once, Runa gave into them. She sniffed and coughed, her body shaking, crying out all the fear and misery.

At last, Runa closed her fists and made herself calm. She had to think.

"A plan," she whispered to herself. "I need a plan."

Her main fear was that she was in tSardia, for that had been her uncle's intended destination. The cold and her tiredness made it hard to think, but she forced herself to run through the facts.

They had only sailed for two days. She was sure her brother Mareq had complained to her once about having to stay on board a ship for three days to reach Leis, the southernmost port of Callenlas. So, if they had only sailed for two days then they could have been wrecked along the east coast of Callenlas, perhaps towards the south as the winds had been in their favour. Dragging from her memory the maps she was supposed to have studied under Master Greigon, Runa recalled that the east coast of Callenlas was almost entirely forest, which would fit with her current location.

A little relief warmed her arms, and she leaned her head back against the solid tree. At least she was safe in Callenlas.

It was a large forest, however, and she had no map. Worst of all, no one was looking for her, except her treacherous uncle.

"What should I do?" Runa asked herself.

She could travel north and hope to reach Feldemoore. She had heard that some people inhabited the forests, descendants of the stars, though some said they were only legendary.

Something was poking her in the stomach. Runa felt about, expecting to find a twig or a thorn. Instead, Uncle Izzecha's jewel stung her hand.

Of course. The weapon.

The plan flooded her mind in an instant. She had no choice. Getting back to her father in Feldemoore would have to wait. She needed to get to King Elior and tell him of Uncle Izzecha's treachery. Who knew how much of her father's plans he had already given to the tSardians? He may even have had knowledge of the Callenlasian tactics and shared them with the enemy too.

Dragging up her very patchy mental map of Callenlas, Runa guessed that Orr, the capital of Callenlas, must lie to the west. If she could only work out which way that was. It could take her several days to reach the plains to the west. If she survived. She was cold and hungry, without food, and with a burning head injury.

Gingerly, Runa reached up and touched the part of her head which still throbbed. She winced as her fingers explored her hair, matted with dried blood, and found a large swelling. It seemed it was just a surface injury, however, and not as deep as Uncle Izzecha's.

At least it was not bleeding any more.

Runa could not light a fire and risk drawing her uncle's attention. He may have found some of the sailors and started searching the forest for her. It was too dark to go any further and her legs felt like wool. She pulled some loose leaves over herself and watched the stars turn overhead while she waited for sleep.

Something her nurse had said to her years ago, while still in the nursery, drifted into her mind. It was nurse who had introduced her to the stories of King Elior, telling them in simplified form to Runa and Mareq, tucked into their beds. King Elior was a star and so could hear Sendings from miles around. He had promised to help Callenlas in her hour of need.

Surely there was no need greater than now, Runa reasoned. She had not been given much instruction in using her mind. Sending required concentration and practice, two things Runa struggled with. But she was desperate.

Closing her eyes, Runa reached inside and felt the burning core of herself, now faint and weak. She drew it up, the last of her strength, and Sent out through the forests, as far as she could, seeking out the King.

King Elior, she Sent. *Help me. I'm lost. I need to find you urgently. Please help.*

She did not know if the Sending reached him, if indeed it had even worked at all. There was no indication that he heard.

ဆ * ဿ

For two days Runa pushed her way through the forest. She worked out which way was west by climbing a tree and looking for the Day-Star that first morning. She used the trick she had read about in one of her books (stolen – no, *borrowed* from King Mabrigas's library), *How I Survived the Wilds of Feldemoore*, by Sir Larenli of Albaran. Look ahead and find a tree in line with the direction you want to travel. Walk to that tree. Check that you are in line with the tree you started at. Then choose another tree to align with and walk to that.

Every so often, Runa would climb another tree and check the Day-Star's position. With a few adjustments, she felt she was doing a good job of keeping herself heading westward, though every time she looked around at the scale of the forest, her spirits sank. Trees spread in every direction, as far as she could see.

She found a stream that first morning and washed the salt water from her clothes and hair. The stories of riders and adventurers helped her, as she remembered some berries and roots that were safe to eat and avoided

137

some that would have poisoned her. She wished she had a bow and arrow or had the time to set a trap for rabbits. But she knew she had to press on despite her hunger. Having no idea what Uncle Izzecha was doing, her best hope was to travel west into Callenlas and find someone who could take her to King Elior.

Exhausted and feeling lost, Runa was pressing doggedly through the bushes when she smelled roasting meat and woodsmoke. At first, she thought it was delirium, until she caught sight of the blue thread of smoke weaving above the trees some way to the south. Runa paused.

She did not want to go out of her way and delay her journey any further. But food would give her strength and she might even be able to beg extra to take with her for the following day. Maybe get some directions. Unless it was Uncle Izzecha ...

In the end, the grumbling of her stomach drove her south, creeping cautiously as she drew nearer.

She could hear voices, adult men talking, over the crackling of the fire. Peering around a tree, Runa could only see two men, one crouching over the flames, the other splitting logs with a large axe. They were strangers, dressed in rough brown and green tunics and trousers – clearly woodsmen and not sailors.

Runa risked stepping out of the trees.

Instantly, both men were on the alert. The one by the fire rose to his feet, the other lifted the axe in his hand as though it were a weapon.

Runa held her hands out, palms forwards. When they saw she was not an adult, they relaxed.

"What be you doin' out here?" the one with the axe asked.

"Are you alone?" the one by the fire asked. He had a thin moustache over his mouth, hair cut close to his head, his eyes sharp and attentive.

"Yes," Runa answered. Her eyes were riveted on the fire where a spit had been constructed to roast what looked like a pheasant, or some other kind of large bird. It was spitting fat and smelled delicious.

"Hungry?" the cook caught the direction of her gaze.

Runa could only nod.

"I reckon we can spare you a wing. Sit here."

The cook rummaged in a leather bag and tossed a hunk of bread to Runa. It was a bit stale, but Runa could not care less. She munched it thankfully as they waited for the bird to finish cooking. She ate as much as they would give her, licking the grease off her fingers and chewing on the bones. She had never felt so hungry.

"Right, now you're fed, tell us a bit about yerself."

The cook was lean and scrawny, his arms all sinew and bone as they reached out to stir the fire.

"I was on board a trade ship," Runa said, deciding to keep the details sketchy in case her uncle came across the men. "We were shipwrecked in the storm. I walked inland, hoping to find help."

"What was a girl doing aboard a trade ship?"

"I was with my father, a trader," Runa said. "Heading south to Leis."

She could tell the man did not believe her, but that could not be helped. She stood, wiping her hands on her tunic.

"Well, thanks," she said. "But I must be on my way."

The cook gave a mirthless chuckle.

"Not so fast," he said. "We can't leave a young lady running about these woods all by herself. There's dangerous men about."

Runa licked her lips.

"At the very least you might pay us for the food we caught and cooked for you."

"Of course. Only, I have no money on me."

"How about that nice dagger? Very pretty that is."

Runa curled her fingers protectively around the silver hilt.

"This is precious to me."

"I can see that. Royal crest, isn't it? And is that amber on the hilt?"

"Not royal," Runa tightened her fist. Her heart was

140

pounding as though she was already running. Could she outpace two men, after two days of fasting?

She had to find out.

Runa had the advantage as she whipped into the trees. She could hear the men struggling off the ground, their feet thudding against the soft earth as they made after her. She ducked and weaved through the trees like a rabbit, but she was unused to the uneven ground and the roots snared her feet. Her ankle twisted badly. She tried to scramble back to her feet but the cook's hand grasped her leg and pulled her backwards.

Runa shrieked with anger and tried to draw her knife, but he was fast, anticipating it, and had the knife in his hand before she did. He pressed the point to her throat, and she sank back against the ground, despondent.

"Please," she begged. "You have to let me go. You don't know …"

She thought of the jewel hidden under her tunic, of the war, of her father, of all the ordinary people in Callenlas and Feldemoore whose futures may rest on her getting her uncle's plot to the right ears. She could not begin to explain and did not want to, for who knew where such a man's loyalties might lie.

The cook was a hard man, and his rough hands yanked Runa upright. He forced her back to the clearing with her own knife and pushed her into a small shed, concealed in the trees.

"We'll decide what to do with you later," he said ominously, before slamming the door shut. Runa heard a heavy bolt slide into place and sank onto the floor in despair.

CHAPTER 15

It was dark in the shed. The only light came in through the narrow gaps between the uneven boards, and the trees grew close about it. Runa sat for a moment, fighting tears, waiting for her eyes to adjust to the gloom. Partly, she was desperate, her desire to reach King Elior frustrated. Partly, she was furious – what kind of a rider gets captured three times in five days?

A shaft of low light came in under the door, spreading across the floor, illuminating the edge of a pottery bowl and cup, lying beside a heap of old blankets. At least there was somewhere to sleep.

Runa's mind whirred with ideas, none very sensible, of how she could escape and get her knife back.

A rasping sound came from the blankets, and she leaped to her feet, pressing her back against the wall. What had they shut her up with?

The blankets moved slightly, and then a hacking

143

cough began, which she first took for a dog's bark.

When nothing emerged from the blankets, Runa reassessed, and realised that it actually sounded like someone very sick. Whatever – whoever – was under those blankets was unlikely to pose a threat. All the same, it took Runa quite a while to find the courage to creep over and pull back the threadbare covers.

It was a boy, lying on his back, his dark hair tumbling over his forehead and around his face in black waves. A thick fringe of black lashes brushed his cheeks and his eyes fluttered beneath the lids. He would be quite handsome, Runa observed, if he was not so dirty and pale. Runa sniffed. And if he did not smell of damp and sweat.

Pity was her first response, for a fellow-prisoner, for someone so sick and helpless. His lips were white and cracked with thirst. Runa reached for the cup, and gingerly lifted his head so that she could give him a few sips of water. There was only a small amount left in the cup and she could not imagine it was fresh. The boy swallowed painfully and licked his lips.

"More," he whispered hoarsely. Runa gave him what was left, then put the cup aside. She wondered how long he had been here, whether the men knew he was sick.

The boy's forehead was burning hot but he pulled the blankets back over himself, falling back to sleep. His pitiable state made Runa angry. She jumped to her feet and hammered on the door.

"The boy in here is sick!" she shouted. "He needs water!"

There was no reply but the rustling of the trees and the chittering of birds. Runa could not even tell if they could hear her.

Ȥ * ȡ

As darkness fell Runa heard footsteps outside the hut. She stood, instantly alert, ready for anything including a fight.

A little hatch at the base of the door slid roughly open, and a plate of food was pushed inside and left on the floor.

"Gimme the other cup and plate," the cook's voice came through the door.

Runa scrambled forward, obedient only because she wanted help.

"I need water, and clean blankets. The boy in here is sick." She shoved the other plate and cup back through the hatch.

"Blankets, water," the man chuckled to himself. "Who do you think you are!"

"It doesn't matter who I am – the boy is sick! He may die!"

"We put him in there to see whether he'd live or not. If he dies, he's one less body to cart south for the flesh trade. If he lives, we'll make a bit of money out of him. Makes no difference to me."

Flesh traders. Runa shuddered.

The hatch was shunted back into place with a thud and the footsteps receded.

Runa felt murderous. How dare they think they had the right to deprive someone of liberty, to *sell* someone, as if they were a chair or a horse! How dare they treat anyone as they had this poor boy?

Eventually, Runa unclenched her fists and knelt to pick up the water. She was very thirsty herself after eating all the salt meat earlier. But the boy was sick. She gave him a few more sips of water and soaked the bread to make it soft, but he would not eat. She ate the bread herself, slowly, more because she wanted to have plenty of strength in case a chance came to run away than because she was hungry. But she was already struggling in her mind with the dilemma of the boy. If a chance came for her to run, could she leave him, knowing he would almost certainly die? Was one life worth the safety of an entire nation?

Runa gave the boy some more water, before wrapping her cloak tightly about herself and trying to sleep on the floor. The riders, guardians and kings in the histories always seemed so certain of what to do. It seemed much harder when you were the person deciding.

ක * ක

Dawn sent the Day-Star's light slanting across the floor of the hut, pouring through the cracks in the eastern wall. Runa rubbed her eyes and looked about, disorientated. Then she remembered and hugged herself tightly.

She patted her chest and felt the unpleasant weight of the jewel still there. The boy was asleep, his breathing shallow and fast. Runa wanted to do more for him and hated feeling so helpless.

A thin porridge and more water were brought that morning. She obsessed over ways to escape as she scooped spoonfuls of the miserable meal into her unwilling mouth.

As the day passed, Runa felt more and more like a caged animal. She even tried to scramble up the walls to try to see through the slight gap between the top of the wall and the roof but could not get a proper foothold.

She paced up and down, shouted threats at the men, uncaring of whether they could hear her or not, and muttered to herself about the laws father would pass and the dire punishments he would level against all flesh traders once she was free.

She was beginning to fear that she would never

escape. She would be tied up and carried south, sold to a tSardian flesh trader. Maybe even taken to the lands over the sea. No one would believe that she was a princess; and even if they did, all they would do was raise her price.

The war would go on; her uncle's plot would succeed and what would become of King Elior's kingdom and Feldemoore?

Runa clenched and unclenched her fist.

"Water," the boy whispered.

She almost did not hear him; she was so lost in her fears. Runa helped him drink, slow sips, then lowered his head to the pillow.

"Am I in tSardia?" the boy asked, his voice rasping. His eyes struggled to focus and kept shifting about the shadows of the hut.

"No," Runa replied. "We're in Callenlas. Are you from tSardia?"

The boy nodded. Runa recoiled. What was a tSardian doing so far north, over the border? Could he have been picked up in tSardia and brought here? It seemed unlikely. Could he be a spy? He was surely too young.

His eyes had rolled back, and he was asleep or unconscious; Runa could not tell. She watched him more closely now, for traces of his story, for what had brought him here. But he just looked like a boy, his dark hair damp with sweat, his skin pale with sickness.

CHAPTER 16

Zaphreth was walking down the long corridor again, the one with the star door at its end. This time, the cheerful Master Filias was not there and he had to face Lord Lur alone.

Zaphreth had been summoned from the practice yard where he had been running through sword drills. Sometimes he joined the ordinary recruits for training; sometimes he had lessons just for the General's Guard. The Masters worked them hard, expecting the king's soldiers to be ready for battle after twelve weeks of training. The General's Guard usually had a longer training period, and Zaphreth was becoming impatient. He had watched troops march north to the battle lines over and again and was eager to be part of the procession, with banners waving and people cheering.

Almost six months had passed since Zaphreth had

first met the General. He had learned every basic sword drill by heart and more; he had stretched himself in Mind Powers again and again with his tutor; he had run countless circuits of the training yard ... Yet still he had received no commission. He was beginning to worry that Lord Lur had forgotten him.

Then, in the middle of his training, one of the General's personal Guard, wearing one of their strange helmets that covered the face in strips of metal leaving only a shadowy eye-slit, came and stood at the edge of the training yard. The Master consulted with him and then called Zaphreth out.

"The General sends for you," the guard said, in a tone-less voice.

Zaphreth laid down his practice sword and stripped off his gloves, following the formidable figure through the barracks and into the palace beyond.

The guard left him at the start of the General's corridor, and Zaphreth made his way down it alone. He felt that same sense of oppression and fear and he began to worry. Why had the General finally asked for him? Had he done something wrong? Or was it finally time for him to be commissioned?

Lord Lur was seated at a table this time, off the dais, busy with maps and scrolls. His face was set in a frown.

"What is it?" he asked, when the door opened and

Zaphreth stepped in. The guards had their spears up again.

"It's me, Lord," Zaphreth said, trying to keep his nervousness from his voice. The General despised anxiety. "Zaphreth of Havara."

"Yes, yes," Lord Lur beckoned him closer, and Zaphreth hurried up the hall to stand before his Lord.

The General wore no robe today, but his silk tunic was the colour of wine, the cuffs and collar stiffly embroidered with gold.

"You are required," Lord Lur said, still glancing through his papers, "for a very important, very secret mission."

"Yes, Lord," Zaphreth said, his heart beating faster at the words 'very important, very secret'.

"I need spies, good spies, who can cross into Callenlas and live undetected among her people. I need men who can get close to their King and find out his plans. I need to know what Elior is doing, I need to know how he sleeps at night, what he eats, when he has a cold, when he is tired."

There was an edge of irritation to Lord Lur's voice, but Zaphreth reasoned that he must have a great deal to worry about. News from the battlelines had not been positive lately – not that anyone in the city had heard of the defeats at Ilath and Berrias.

"Your skill with Mind Powers should enable you to do this task. Certainly, Sending information to me will not tax you as it would another.

"I have arranged for a guide to take you to a place where the border can be crossed without trouble. You will go to the camp where their so-called King is and sign up to serve him. Become a squire, or something. Send as much information as you can get to me. Understand?"

Zaphreth blustered. The commission was so sudden, so unexpected, and so full of risk and vagueness that he did not know what to say.

The clerk at Lord Lur's elbow stared at him, eyes wide with horror, and it was only when Lord Lur finally raised his dark eyes to glare impatiently at Zaphreth that he found words to spill out.

"I am your servant, my Lord," he stammered. "I will go. But ..."

The clerk's face paled, and a dangerous glint appeared in the General's eye.

"My Lord, please, forgive me, but ... if anything happens to me in the North ... My mother, she is all alone."

Lur looked at Zaphreth, his dark eyes narrowing as though he was struggling to comprehend the concern.

"Your mother will be honoured for her sacrifice to me, to King Lakesh, and to her people," he said eventually.

"She has no one to provide for her, Lord."

"Ah." Lur nodded, but Zaphreth had no confidence that he understood at all, or that he had absorbed the problem.

"If my wages could go to her while I am away ...?" Zaphreth suggested.

"You," Lord Lur waved his quill at the clerk. "Make a note of his mother's name. Ensure his wages go to her."

The clerk gulped a reply and the General lowered his head back to his desk.

"Forgive me," Zaphreth tried again. "Am I to go as myself?"

A gusty sigh from the General fluttered all the papers and Zaphreth felt the air around him pulse. He was sure he could feel some pressure on his throat, as though Lord Lur was compressing his windpipe with Mind Powers. But he was not about to go into Callenlas without clearer instruction.

"Who else would you go as?" Lord Lur asked.

"I mean, Lord, as far as anyone knows, I am just a poor apprentice. Why should King Elior, as he calls himself, allow me close to him?"

The General looked at Zaphreth, his eyes black apart from two pinpoints of light. Zaphreth swallowed hard.

"You are a smart boy," the General said. "I will leave the details to you to smooth out, but I would go as yourself. As Lord of Talivera, I mean. That is one of the lands belonging to Prince Herodas."

Zaphreth's heart swelled – as heir to Prince Herodas, how many lands would be his? But innumerable problems and questions flooded his mind, spoiling the moment.

"I have no money, Lord. A penniless Lord is not going to be very convincing."

The General opened a drawer under the table and tossed a pouch of fine leather and Zaphreth. It clinked as it landed in his hands.

"That should be sufficient. Now go!"

Zaphreth managed to leave the hall and the General's presence with dignity, but once beyond the stone door, he skipped and tossed the bag up and down in his hand, feeling the weight of more money than he had ever held in his life. Before he left the palace, he eased open the neck of the pouch. The coin within reflected the gold of the Day-Star.

But Zaphreth stepped out of the palace not into the barracks, but onto the desert sand. Wirrat's laughing face passed in front of Zaphreth and he was tossing the pouch of gold up and down in his hand. Zaphreth reached out to snatch back his gold, but Wirrat's dark face grimaced. He slid the pouch into his cloak. Zaphreth wanted to protest, but a figure stood in the distance, cloak flying in the wind, his face in shadow. His sword was raised menacingly and he was coming at Zaphreth.

Turning to run, Zaphreth's feet slipped in the sand. He could hear the figure bearing down on him, blade flashing. King Elior? Or Lord Lur? He could not tell. All he felt was fear, fear for his life, fear for ... Ama. He had to protect Ama. But she was weeping round the corner. He could hear her sobs. Now he could see her stricken face.

It was more than he could bear. Zaphreth woke with a shout, sitting up suddenly.

Yet he still could not find his bearings. It was dark, he was too hot, too thirsty. And he did not know where he was.

A pale face, just shadows for features in the half-light, hovered in front of him. A soft voice spoke in a strange accent. A girl, he realised.

"I'm Runa," she was saying. "What's your name?"

"Zaphreth," he managed to breathe.

"Lie down, Zaphreth," she urged him. "You were having a dream."

It had seemed real, he thought. Some of it had been. But he lay down obediently and sipped the water she brought.

His eyes were adjusting to the dim light now and he could see the four walls crowded around them, the door without inner handle or bolt and the filtered forest light slipping through the cracks in the walls. He could see the girl, moving around the beaten-earth floor in

155

a crouch, her hair as bright as the great copper pans in the barracks' kitchens. When she turned to look at him again, he saw that her eyes were green, her nose smattered with freckles.

"How did you end up here?" she was asking.

Zaphreth's mind was foggy, as if he had drunk too much ale, or the fire-syrup that Wirrat was so fond of. He remembered that it was a secret ... something was ... he had to get to King Elior.

"I'm from tSardia," he mumbled. "I'm a prince. Very important. I must find King Elior."

Runa stopped what she was doing and looked more closely at him.

"You're a prince?" she asked, with more than an edge of incredulity.

"Yes!" Zaphreth asserted. It was very important that she understood this.

"Oh," Runa smiled. "You're delirious!"

"No!" Zaphreth felt intensely annoyed. "My father is – was – Prince Herodas of tSardia. I'm in disguise, so that I could get over the border."

"Why would a prince of tSardia want to cross the border into Callenlas? Apart from to spy, of course."

"Not a spy," Zaphreth shook his head, which made the room spin. "I'm detefting ... decef ... cedefting."

"Defecting?" Runa spoke slowly, patiently. This

156

annoyed Zaphreth even more.

"Yes. Defecting. I want to join King Elior. I thought he might receive me if I offered him information."

"I'm not sure he will want you," Runa said, primly. "I mean, you're a tSardian. And I don't think offering to betray your own people would make you look any better in his eyes. You could be a double-crossing spy. Though I think a spy might be cleverer than to get caught by flesh traders. Here." She offered him a spoonful of bread soaked in water.

Zaphreth accepted it, with the insult, but worked on his reply while he chewed.

"You got caught by them too."

Runa inclined her head, with a rueful twist of her mouth.

"True."

"I'm a trained soldier," Zaphreth added, eager to prove his suitability to work for King Elior.

"A soldier?" Runa exclaimed. "But you're only a boy!"

"I'm fourteen," Zaphreth retorted, defensively. "I'm considered a man in tSardia."

"Well, in Feldemoore," Runa replied, "we don't allow anyone to fight until they are eighteen. And I think Callenlas has the same law."

"You're from Feldemoore? I thought you were Callenlasian."

"No. I was shipwrecked off the coast, and then got picked up by the traders."

"Bad luck."

"It's embarrassing, is what it is," Runa replied, pulling a face. "I am sure King Elior will at least hear your story," she continued. "He is wise and kind. Not like your tSardian rulers. I'm not surprised you wanted to leave."

"Have you met him, then?" Zaphreth managed to ignore her rudeness about his homeland.

"No," Runa admitted. "But I have read many stories of his deeds over the centuries. And Fa— our king thinks highly of him. King Mabrigas."

"So, you believe the stories then? That stars live among people?"

"You don't?" Runa seemed surprised.

Zaphreth hesitated, considering his response. He could hardly retort that he thought they were all children's stories.

"We are taught they are false. That King Elior is only human, perhaps a succession of human kings who take the same name to ensure the continuation of the legend, and to keep their power."

Runa looked shocked.

"How would that work?" she exclaimed. "Everyone would know! You can't have one person be king one day and then another person the next, and no one notice."

"Well, of course, the other leaders would be in on the deception."

"There is no deception. If you want to be on King Elior's side, you have to believe in him."

Zaphreth was baffled by her determination to believe such improbable stories, but fatigue was overcoming him again.

"You must rest," Runa said, with a matronly air. Zaphreth did not argue. It was making his head spin trying to hold all his threads of thought together: his desire to refute Runa's nonsensical belief in the immortality of Elior, yet needing to appear loyal to the King, while suppressing his true love for tSardia and Lord Lur ... Zaphreth gladly closed his eyes and slept.

৪১ ✳ ৫৪

"How did you get here?" Zaphreth asked, later in the evening. He could see her tunic; it was faded and ragged in patches, but it had once been a fine garment.

"My father is a merchant; our ship got wrecked three, maybe four nights ago." Runa paused and glanced at Zaphreth before continuing her story with some hesitancy. "My father stayed with the broken ship, to guard his merchandise and wait for our rescue ship. He sent me overland with an important gift for King Elior.

I'm heading for the capital – " here Runa's voice trailed as her eyes flitted over the walls of the shed. "If I can get away from the flesh traders, that is," she concluded, glumly.

Well, here was luck, thought Zaphreth, though he revealed nothing of the surprise and hope that lit up his mind at Runa's revelation. He had fallen in with someone heading for his very destination. He would have to get on her good side. It would be no end of help to have someone to travel with, someone with a reason to enter the King's house at Orr, and perhaps – Zaphreth hardly dared to put the hope into words in his head – perhaps even introduce him to King Elior.

"I could break us out of here with Mind Powers," he said, casually, flexing his fingers as if to test their strength. "When I'm a bit stronger, anyway."

"You mean the gift?" Runa leaned forward with interest, and Zaphreth sighed internally. He should have kept that quiet, he thought. This girl might not think through the consequences, but someone of a military mindset would surely realise that someone with strong Mind Powers could Send information back to tSardia.

Zaphreth shrugged.

"We call them Powers in tSardia."

"It is the gift of the stars," Runa answered, with reverence. Zaphreth bit back a sigh of scorn.

"Did you travel much, with your father?" he asked, changing the subject, before he gave away too much of his scepticism. She was clearly rather naïve, trusting him to be truthful as well as believing the stories about Elior. But he would have to be very careful not to give himself away; he was still feeling feverish and did not fully trust his mind to remember his mission at all times. If she guessed his true aim, Runa might well suffocate him while he slept.

"Only up and down the coast of Callenlas and Feldemoore," Runa replied, picking at a loose thread on one of her shoes.

"Did you hear much about the war?"

Runa glanced at him. Zaphreth kept his face expressionless.

"Sometimes," she said. "But Feldemoore isn't fighting yet, so we don't hear that much."

"Yet?" Zaphreth asked, trying to keep his tone innocuous. "Are Feldemoore planning to join the war?"

Runa shrugged, apparently bored with the conversation.

"I don't know much about politics," she said. "Being just a merchant's daughter. Why did you join the army?"

Zaphreth blinked at the abrupt change of subject. He tried to think of a motive she would believe.

"I was a prince. I was expected to."

"Did you enjoy using a sword?" Runa asked, a glint of interest in her green eyes.

"It wasn't really my strength," Zaphreth replied, uncomfortable at discussing truths about his life. "I was better with Mind Powers."

"My brothers used to teach me to fight, but then they grew up. And my governesses said it wasn't appropriate for a pr ... for a lady."

"Do they teach you Mind Powers in Feldemoore? I mean, the gift?" the silly term stuck in Zaphreth's throat, but he supposed he would have to speak more and more like a Callenlasian if his story was to be believed.

"I can barely make a light," Runa admitted ruefully. "I wasn't very good at attending to my lessons."

"It's not difficult," Zaphreth replied.

"I've read about some Masters who could throw a wave of force against their enemies and knock them to the floor!"

"Well, it's possible, but one step at a time!" Zaphreth laughed suddenly. "If you try to do too much you'll just collapse. It's like trying to lift a hundred weight without working up to it. You have to train the mind, just like a muscle."

"So, train me!"

Zaphreth found himself grinning at her. No one had ever taken so much notice of him before; he was the

162

poor apprentice, the bottom of society. He wondered how she would treat him if she knew the truth, that he had not two coppers to rub together, and certainly no lands or title. Still, he might as well get used to behaving like a noble. Soon it would be a reality.

He pulled himself up a little on his mat. Teaching Runa a few mind tricks would help pass the time, and perhaps make her feel that she owed him something. The last thing he wanted was her heading for the hills if he broke open the door, leaving him to find his own miserable way across Callenlas.

"I won't be able to demonstrate," he said. "I'm still too weak. So, you'll just have to listen and try to do what I say."

"If you get tired, just say," Runa said, as she scoured the hut for something suitable to practise on. She took up the empty water bowl and set it in the middle of the floor, then sat cross-legged, looking at Zaphreth expectantly.

"You'll never lift that first try," Zaphreth said, with more than a hint of superiority.

Runa pulled a face to show her annoyance at his tone, but found a straw, and placed it on the beaten earth in front of her. Despite her instructor's arrogance, she felt a flutter of excitement at the thought of finally learning something useful.

CHAPTER 17

Runa lay on her back, watching the slats of light change as the Day-Star rose somewhere beyond the trees, somewhere beyond the sea. As she had done every night and morning since she was washed ashore, Runa Sent a message of desperation to Elior, or to anyone who might hear it, but it was a half-hearted Sending. She had no confidence that anyone would be nearby, and after three nights in the hut, her hope was at its lowest ebb.

Zaphreth mumbled in his sleep. Runa turned to consider his profile, dimly lit by the morning light. His nose was straight and pointed, his eyelashes thick and dark on high cheekbones. With his hair off his face and without the daylight showing his pallor, Zaphreth was quite handsome. And his eyes ... Runa had never seen anyone with such dark blue eyes.

Runa wondered what to make of his boasting,

apart from the displeasure it awoke in her. Her initial compassion had worn thin pretty quickly as Zaphreth had gone on about his skill in Mind Powers and clearly thought being a prince made him special. Runa had far too much experience of people who thought their position made them special, but her natural instinct was to trust, especially someone so weak and far from home. But why would a prince of tSardia, with lands and money and power, leave it all to join King Elior?

Now Runa curled on her side, misery washing over her like the waves of the sea. She had left a palace. She had run away from privilege and comfort. Perhaps he had been as lonely and as unhappy as she had been.

She wondered if her father was missing her now. She should have arrived in Lelanta three days ago. Perhaps they thought her ship had been delayed. Perhaps they were frantically scouring the north coast of Feldemoore for a wreck. The Dragon's Wing was notoriously dangerous to sail around, though in summer it should not have been too difficult.

Zaphreth's eyes flickered open. The frown had gone from his face and he looked a little better.

After sharing the bowl of porridge that was thrust through the door, Zaphreth began looking around the hut.

"My bag ..." he said, as if just remembering. "I had a pack."

"There's nothing else here," Runa replied.

"It doesn't really matter," Zaphreth sighed, sinking back against the wall of the hut. "My money was stolen anyway."

"Who stole it?" Runa demanded, her sense of injustice flaring.

"Someone in a tavern," Zaphreth mumbled. "I left my pack for a moment and when I came back it was gone."

"I'm sorry," Runa said, earnestly. For all his pride, it must have been horrible to realise that all his money was gone.

"What made you leave?" she asked softly, crossing her legs, and settling back on her blanket.

"Leave?"

"Leave tSardia. Leave your home, your family?"

There was a long pause. Zaphreth closed his eyes and leaned his head back against the wall and Runa chewed on her lip. She had not meant to pry.

"I was unhappy," Zaphreth said, in a small voice, which made Runa think that maybe he was not such an idiot after all. "The war was damaging my country. The king was not leading well and we had started to lose some battles. I thought ... I thought maybe King Elior might be right."

Runa looked at Zaphreth with new consideration. People were such puzzles, she decided.

"What about your family?" she asked, thinking of her father, buried behind his piles of paperwork, meeting with ambassadors and officials, appeasing councillors and Masters. "Will they miss you?"

"It's complicated," Zaphreth said, in an even smaller voice.

The tSardian prince, skilled in Mind Arts, turned onto his side and put his back to Runa. She decided not to notice the shaking of his shoulders or the muffled sniffing.

When Zaphreth had slept and woken again, Runa got him to sit up and teach her more of the gift. She was able to make quite a steady light in her palm now, a faintly green edge to its pale glow. Moving things was trickier. She was growing frustrated at the twig which remained stubbornly fixed to the floor, however hard she tried to move it.

"You have to relax," Zaphreth kept insisting, the amusement in his voice far from helpful. "The harder you try the harder it will be. You don't try hard to lift your arm, do you?"

"I can see my arm!! And I've been moving it since I was a baby! This is different."

"Not really," Zaphreth argued. "It's just pushing your

167

power outside your body."

Runa folded her arms and squinted at the stick again. Suddenly it lifted, spiralling up into the middle of the hut, where it danced and span.

Runa gasped and sat back. For a brief moment she thought she had done it, then doubt set in. She glanced at Zaphreth. She could barely tell from his face, but his eyes kept flickering at the twig, and she knew it was him.

"Hey!" she exclaimed, thumping his leg. He gasped and let the stick fall.

"Sorry," Runa said. "I forgot you were ill."

Zaphreth shrugged, rubbing his shin. "I feel a bit stronger now," he said.

"Perhaps you should stand up and try to walk."

Zaphreth shifted himself around awkwardly and pushed up with his hands. Runa gripped his upper arm and tried to help him, but he soon collapsed back onto the bed, defeated.

"Don't worry," Runa tried to reassure him. "You're getting stronger all the time."

But inside she was anxious. Every night that passed brought them closer to being carted south for sale, taking away the hope that she would ever be free again, let alone take her warning to King Elior.

৪৹ ✳ ଓଃ

Runa woke in the darkness. She listened to Zaphreth's breathing, wondering if he was awake too, but he was sleeping peacefully at last.

The sense of the four walls close about her made her feel fearful, so she closed her eyes again and pretended she was sleeping out in the open, a sky rider on an adventure in the service of King Elior. She pretended that the trees stretched above her, their branches and leaves dark shadows against the rich blue of the night sky, jewelled with dancing stars. She felt their gaze on her, but having had a few days to think, she now shrank from their sight.

Runa wrestled with a feeling of despondency. She was not worthy of being a rider. The stars watched humans, and they had seen her disobey her father and her tutors. They had seen her make trouble, deliberately, by running away. They had seen her neglect her duty as a princess.

All her short life, Runa had wanted nothing more than to stand before King Elior and be accepted into his service, to train to become a sky rider in his cohort of dragons. She had always known it was an unrealistic dream. She was a Feldemoorian, for a start. She had responsibilities as a princess to her own nation, such as marrying and making an alliance with a foreign nation.

The admittedly small hope that it might just be possible, had never quite left her, like a light in the window of a distant house, guiding her through the night. But now she could see her own unworthiness and her dream seemed to be crumbling before her. King Elior would see right through her. He would see her laziness, her refusal to work, her refusal to obey.

And father would never allow it now. She would be sent straight to Lelanta, she had no doubt of that. All she had done in the last few days was confirm her father's opinion of her – she was a troublemaker, not only causing trouble for herself, but for her father and his entire kingdom.

Shouting and scuffling outside made Runa start. She pulled her cloak about her, wishing it was not so dark. A bright flash from outside cast a momentary light through the gaps in the boards, then the hut was plunged back into darkness.

"What was that?" Zaphreth hissed.

"No idea. Better be ready to run. Do you think you can get far?"

Zaphreth made no answer but grunted as he pushed aside the blankets and stood, swaying a little.

"Why are you wearing a dress?" Runa asked suddenly, peering at him in the half-light.

"Do you really want to worry about that now?" Zaphreth asked.

"The short answer," she nodded.

"I was afraid of being captured. This is my disguise."

Runa grinned widely in the darkness.

"You look very pretty," she said.

Another flash lit up the shed and revealed the fear in both of their faces.

"We'll run together," she said decisively. "It's dark; it'll be easy to find somewhere to hide."

Zaphreth nodded, and Runa's stomach turned over in fear for him. He was pale and swaying on his feet. Could they really outrun whatever or whoever was out there?

But the boy's jaw was set firmly in a determination Runa recognised in herself. She gripped his hand as the noises grew nearer.

"I think I have the strength to break the door open," Zaphreth said.

"Don't exhaust yourself," Runa cautioned, but Zaphreth was already raising his fist.

He threw his hand forwards, opening his fingers as though releasing a ball. The door burst off its hinges with a bang and they sprinted together, running around the hut and into the thick trees.

Branches whipped Runa in the face, and she stumbled over roots and snagging vines. But Zaphreth was with her, urging her on, their hands wound tightly together. Shouts came from behind them, and running feet, but Runa had learned her lesson and would not look back.

Zaphreth was tiring. Runa could feel his weight slowing her. His breathing was laboured.

Runa held out her palm and Sent out light momentarily to help her see the way. There must be somewhere they could hide, a large bush, or a hollow tree ... But from the trees in front three figures emerged, cloaked in shadowy green. Runa tried to weave around them but they were too many. Strong arms wrapped around her, separating her from Zaphreth.

"No!" she shrieked, enraged and despairing at the same moment. "No – you must let me go!" She bucked and fought with all her desperate strength.

"Hush, hush, you're safe now," the figures tried to reassure her, but still she fought.

"No, you don't understand – I must get away! I must!"

"You *are* away. We are the King's servants, working against the flesh trade."

Runa finally paused. "You are the King's servants?"

The man holding her relaxed slightly but did not let her go. Another came to stand in front of her, drawing back his hood so that she could see his face in the low light. His eyes met hers.

"We are. We do his business in bringing an end to the flesh trade."

"I'm also on the King's business," Runa tried to speak calmly.

The supposed rescuers chuckled, and Zaphreth stared at her.

"I have an urgent message for King Elior," Runa insisted. "I must reach him without delay."

"And who, pray, entrusted such a vital message to a little girl?" asked a fourth man, emerging from the trees. He drew back his cloak, revealing a neat beard and rather pointed features. He reminded Runa a great deal of a fox, though his hair was brown.

"I am not a little girl," Runa replied. "I am thirteen!"

"How long have you been imprisoned?" this time a woman spoke, her voice kind. Her hair was the colour of wheat under the moon and hung long down her back.

"Three nights," Runa replied. "I was lost and hungry – the men gave me food. I didn't know they were traders. Now please, let me go; show me which way and I will walk."

"You need food and rest first," the woman said.

"No," Runa folded her arms, though her body was trembling with fatigue. "My message is urgent, I tell you. It could affect the entire outcome of the war. I've already been stuck in that hut for three days! I will walk all day and night, even if it kills me. I must reach the King tomorrow!"

The fox and the woman exchanged glances filled with curiosity and a disbelief that made Runa's blood boil.

"I'm afraid you will not reach the King tomorrow," the woman said. "He is at the southern border, leading the defence against tSardia. It would take a week or more to reach him on foot, even if you walked all the hours of daylight."

Runa's heart sank. Until now, the hope that had driven her was that Orr could not be far away – her geography lessons had taught her that much. It was only a short journey from the edge of the forest. But if the King was not in Orr her quest was futile and all her efforts had been in vain. She sank to the ground. Her uncle would reach tSardia; they would surely have ways to recreate the weapon or find alternatives. And he would prevent father from entering the war and all would be lost; Callenlas would be overtaken and everything good and beautiful would be gone.

"I am Bran, governor of Iliatharnae," the fox said. "If you give me your message, I will Send it for you."

Runa shook her head, drawing shaky breaths as she fought for self-control. She sniffed and wiped her eyes.

"No," she said. "I cannot trust anyone. It must be me."

They spoke briefly to one another in hushed voices. Then they turned to Runa and the woman pronounced their verdict.

"If you will eat and drink now, then I will travel with you to the edge of the forest. Sky riders are stationed around the country to carry messages and to offer protection. I am sure we will be able to find one to carry you south to the battle lines."

"A dragon will take me?" Runa asked, stunned.

"You don't need to be afraid," Bran said, misreading Runa's emotion. "The dragon will obey its rider absolutely. And you are only small – you will not impede its flight."

"No," Runa could hardly speak. "It is my dream to ride a dragon!"

The rescuers brought food from their bags and gave some to Runa. Now that the need to fight had faded, a profound tiredness came over her. She sank back against a tree trunk and fought the urge to sleep.

"Perhaps you had better sleep for a few hours," the woman said, frowning.

"No!" that was enough to drive Runa upright again.

"What will happen to Zaphreth?" Runa asked, glancing at her friend. He had fallen asleep and now seemed pale and small under the boughs of a great spreading oak.

"Who is he?" Bran asked.

"He's a tSardian prince," Runa explained. "He ran away from their army. They make them fight once they are fourteen! He wants to pledge allegiance to King Elior, if he is allowed, or at least to take shelter here until the war is over."

"You trust him?" Bran asked, raising one eyebrow in

an expression that somehow exaggerated his fox-like appearance.

"I think he should be taken to the King, if possible," Runa answered. "And he helped me escape."

Bran nodded thoughtfully.

"If you can delay just a little, Astara might be able to strengthen him to travel with you."

The woman knelt beside Zaphreth, feeling his head for a fever and flitting over his body, as if searching for something in the air around him.

"He is recovering from a fever," she said. "And has just expended a great deal of power through the gift. I think I can help with that, at least."

Runa watched wearily as Astara laid her hand over Zaphreth's forehead and closed her eyes.

"What are you doing?" Runa asked, with a twinge of anxiety for her new friend.

"Astara is a skilled healer," Bran replied, offering Runa a flask of water. "She is lending some of her strength to Zaphreth. He will be able to travel with you then."

Within moments, Zaphreth blinked and opened his eyes. He lay still for a moment beneath Astara's pale hands, but Runa could see, even in the dim light held in the palms of their rescuers, that his face was brighter. When Astara sat back and opened her eyes, Zaphreth slowly rose. His gaze was clearer, his jaw relaxed. He moved his arms about, as if surprised to find he could move without difficulty.

"Better?" Astara asked with a smile.

"Thank you," Zaphreth said, seeming a bit bewildered by the healing. Runa felt a surge of awe at Astara's ability to heal and wished she had paid more attention in lessons. Perhaps being a healer was not as exciting as being a sky rider, but it was undeniably useful.

"Here, chew on these," Astara drew some herbs from a bag at her hip. "They are not very nice, but they'll help with the fever."

Zaphreth accepted the herbs with a glance of suspicion at Runa. She understood his suspicion, for he was, after all, in the hands of his country's enemies.

"They are friends," she reassured him. "They work for King Elior against the flesh trade."

"Sir, we found these." Another cloaked rescuer approached carrying a handful of objects in a loose sack. Bran sorted through them – there was the battered cooking pan, a spoon, a flint, and –

"My knife!" Runa exclaimed, as the dagger caught the light. Bran lifted it carefully from the other things, examining it by the light he produced in his palm.

"Is this the crest of Feldemoore?" he asked, peering at it. He glanced sharply at Runa.

"It was my mother's," Runa said, reaching for it

protectively. She had thought never to see it again.

"Who are you, exactly?" Bran asked, narrowing his eyes at her.

Runa debated internally. She wanted to trust these people; they had been so kind and had promised so much help. But explanations would cost her time and perhaps even the freedom to travel to the King herself. Runa knew only too well how protective people suddenly became once they realised a princess was among them.

"My mother was an assistant to the Queen of Feldemoore," she said in the end, the lie stinging her lips. "Before she died."

Bran seemed to accept her answer and handed the knife to Runa, who fastened it immediately to her belt. She patted her chest one more time to check that Uncle Izzecha's jewel was still there, then got to her feet.

"We must go," she said.

CHAPTER 18

Zaphreth's feelings were far more tumultuous than Runa's. He had been near to collapse even before their rescuers caught hold of them, and his grasp of Runa's revelation had been foggy at best. As she talked with the cloaked strangers, he had fallen into a half-sleep, half-faint, and then been vaguely conscious of a soothing warmth settling over his entire body. Astara's healing drew him back to consciousness like a gentle rousing from sleep, and he found himself gazing round at the gift-lighted trees with a dazed pleasure. How good it felt to be freed from the trembling exhaustion of fever.

"Here," Bran crouched before Zaphreth and offered him a soft bread roll. Zaphreth took it, nodding his thanks.

"So, what is a tSardian prince doing north of the border? And wearing such a pretty dress?" Bran held no hostility in his voice, and even allowed a friendly, teasing grin to cross his face as he mentioned Zaphreth's disguise. Nevertheless, Bran's grey eyes were fixed on him, and Zaphreth knew it would take all his skill with Mind Powers to resemble a truth-teller. Unlike Runa, Bran's gaze held the sharpness of suspicion, though his voice remained friendly.

"I ran away," he replied, through a mouthful of bread.

"From the army?"

"Yes."

"You are only a boy. Thirteen? Fourteen?"

"Fourteen," Zaphreth replied, taking another bite. It was easier to hide his thoughts with the distraction of food between his mind and Bran's, and he was grateful for the darkness cloaking his gestures and feelings.

"Do boys routinely sign up to fight?" Bran asked.

"Not usually, but it is permitted. My family wanted me to. I am a prince of tSardia."

Bran raised an eyebrow.

"You did not find the army to your liking?"

"It was harsh. And I quickly lost faith in our cause." Zaphreth found this part easier to say than he had expected. "The war no longer seemed just."

"So, you left behind family? Friends? Comrades in arms?"

"A mother. No one else."

Zaphreth found tears pricking his eyes as he thought of Ama. He blinked and swallowed them down.

"Will she be punished for your desertion?" The concern in Bran's voice drew Zaphreth's eyes upwards. Bran's brows were knit in an expression of genuine concern for a woman he had never met, an enemy, miles away, whom he would most likely never meet. It flustered Zaphreth, and a flash of memory, unwanted, played in his mind: of Lur's incomprehension of Zaphreth's worry for his mother.

"I ... I don't think so," Zaphreth replied, in the end.

"What do you plan to do now? You are an enemy soldier." Bran offered Zaphreth a flask of water, another useful distraction which Zaphreth accepted.

"I hoped to serve King Elior," Zaphreth ducked his head, as though this option would be unlikely. He wanted to appear eager but humble also, with the confidence of a nobleman, yet aware of his position as an enemy.

"Only men of eighteen and older are permitted to fight in King Elior's army," Bran replied.

"I didn't mean ... I thought I could carry messages, that sort of thing."

Bran was watching him again, his eyes narrowed. Zaphreth took a drink from the flask.

"King Elior is kind," Bran said. "I am sure he will want to help you. However, you cannot expect to be trusted, not at least until the war is over."

Zaphreth nodded.

"I understand," he said.

"I've a mind to send you to Orr," Bran said, glancing over his shoulder at Runa, who waited impatiently with Astara. "To await King Elior until after the war. You'll be treated well there, have no fear. Like all tSardian captives, you'll be kept secure but comfortable until the war is over and then allowed to choose to return home or swear fealty to the King."

Zaphreth raised astonished eyes to Bran.

"That is what King Elior does with prisoners of war?" he asked.

"Yes."

Zaphreth's visions of his father ailing in a dank cell crumbled. His heart crumbled too.

"The King will not execute the prisoners if he is victorious?"

"No," Bran replied slowly. "I know such a practice will seem strange to you. We know of the tSardian cruelty. It is no surprise to me that you have deserted."

Zaphreth wrestled with himself for a few heartbeats, unable to get past the surge of hope and wonder that his father was almost certainly alive, and, by the mercy of King Elior, well and perhaps even hopeful of coming home. He was also floored by the new and startling realisation that King Elior was merciful and kind. Not the terrorising leader he had been led to imagine.

Zaphreth swallowed a few times, trying to remember his mission. Lur promised freedom. He rubbed the scar in his palm. How could he persuade Bran to send him to the border instead of to Orr?

"Are you strong enough to walk now?" Runa asked, as if on cue.

"I think so ..." Zaphreth said.

"I am wondering if our tSardian friend ought to go to Orr, to wait with his people," Bran said, standing up and addressing Runa.

"Oh," Runa's obvious disappointment was pleasing to Zaphreth. He got to his feet and offered her an awkward smile.

"Perhaps I'd better do as Bran says," he said. If he appeared compliant, Bran was less likely to suspect him of anything. A pang of guilt at his deceit caught him by surprise.

"Please, let him come with me," Runa said. "I did say I would take him to the King when we escaped. You wouldn't want me to break my word."

"No," Bran scratched his jaw.

"Phaelon is nearby," Astara interjected, having Sent to any riders in the region. "If we leave now, we could reach him by the quarter-day."

Bran exhaled, glancing at Zaphreth once more.

"Go on then," he nodded, then grinned abruptly at Zaphreth, humour glinting in his sharp eyes. "But let me give you a tunic first. You're fortunate I have one in my bag."

Zaphreth accepted the tunic awkwardly, feeling discomforted by the kindness of strangers when he was working so hard to deceive them. He almost wished Bran had listened to his better instincts and sent him to Orr, but that was a foolish thought, he told himself impatiently. In fact, as he hastily stripped off the filthy dress, and replaced it with Bran's spare, oversized tunic, his scar burned, and he knew he must Send to Lur at the first opportunity.

"That's better," Bran approved, as Zaphreth straightened the green tunic and nodded his thanks. The hem skimmed his knees and the garment hung loosely on Zaphreth's slight frame. But anything was better than looking like a farm girl.

"Here — you'll be glad of this on the dragon," Bran said, offering Zaphreth a cloak.

"Dragon," Zaphreth repeated, dazed. He had been vaguely aware of the discussion about finding a dragon but now it registered that he would actually be expected to climb onto a scaly back and be born over a mile into the air. Perhaps he would prefer to go to Orr after all! In tSardia only expert riders ever rode dragons, and it was notoriously dangerous. Zaphreth found himself getting to his feet and stumbling through the slowly lightening forest towards the plains in the west, battling his fear of dragons which rose in pitch with every step against the unwillingness to look like a coward. For Runa seemed excited at the thought of riding the scaly, uneven back of the most dangerous creature known to man.

He clenched his fists and fought his fear. If he went by dragon, he would reach King Elior all the sooner, and could Send even more useful information to Lord Lur. This was what he had wanted, to stick with Runa until he had at least found a way to join King Elior's service.

Walking through the forest a few paces behind Runa, Zaphreth forced himself to think. Lord Lur would be wondering what had happened to him. He was not quite sure how long he had spent in captivity; five days at least. He had vague impressions of travelling by cart for a long time after the flesh traders picked him up and his fever really took hold. He knew he ought to Send to Lur. At the very least his location, but also the news that Runa was making her way rapidly south with information that could affect the war.

Her revelation had caught him by surprise, and he glanced at her with a renewed sense of curiosity. Now that he considered her again, instead of dismissing her as lost and slightly annoying, he felt he ought not to have been surprised. Runa was different from the (admittedly few) other girls he had spent time with. She was dynamic, purposeful. She would make stuff happen and would fight the things that tried to happen to her. Watching her stride through the grass and forest plants, talking eagerly with Astara, her coppery hair hanging in a tangle down her back, Zaphreth felt a grudging admiration of her ability to deceive him, even as it clashed with an irrational annoyance at her success. If he was to be a spy, surely he needed to be able to see through the deception of others.

Zaphreth pressed his lips together. He wondered how she had come across her information. A trader's daughter, she had said. Perhaps another passenger on board the ship had betrayed foreign secrets. Perhaps her father was a supporter of the war, encouraging Feldemoore into joining King Elior's side. He wished she had told him what she knew.

But, then again, he wished she had not said anything at all because now that Zaphreth was working himself up to Send to Lur, knowing it would take all the strength he had, he did not want to. Runa's crooked grin and freckled nose kept drifting into his mind, and those vivid eyes that looked straight into his. She had been kind to him, he realised, giving him all the water they had, knowing he was an enemy. She had wanted him to live, even when she knew he was tSardian, even before he had told her his story about wanting to swear allegiance to Elior. She had been annoyingly prim at times and was stubborn in her veneration of the oppressive King Elior, but he felt a strange sense of protection towards her and a grudging admiration of her bravery.

His lie of wanting to serve King Elior now made him squirm, but he shoved his conscience down, willing it to be quiet. The scar on his palm also burned. His allegiance lay with Lur. And even though the behaviour of the northerners belied all that he had been taught about this land, Zaphreth had sworn an oath. Lur offered freedom. And, as kind as Runa and Bran had been, they trusted in King Elior, who robbed men of freedom and oppressed the south. Follow him or suffer, seemed to be his motto.

Right now, Runa was doing Zaphreth a favour, distracting Astara, while two other rescuers formed a front and rear guard for their small party. So, he drew a deep breath and Sent his mind south, seeking Lur's presence. It hovered like a cloud many miles to the south, so far that Zaphreth could hardly reach it. He was feeling dizzy and faint, about to give up, when Lur's eye turned upon him.

Lur was probing his mind with that same traumatising piercing that he had experienced in Sarreia.

You have news? Lur asked, his voice heavy in Zaphreth's

mind.

Yes, Lord, Zaphreth Sent.

It was easier this way, with Lur crossing the miles between them, though he could still feel it sapping his strength.

Where have you been? Lur asked, and Zaphreth felt his scar stinging, as though Lord Lur was prodding it to remind him of what he owed.

I was detained by flesh traders, and sick.

Your news?

Zaphreth did not know why he had imagined Lord Lur would care about his plight; of course, he had far more important things to worry about.

There is a girl carrying a message to King Elior. It seems important.

What is the message?

I don't know.

Find out.

Zaphreth felt Lord Lur's impatience like a purple weight in his mind. He struggled under it, as if Lur was pushing him down into the earth.

I am going south ... to pledge my allegiance to King Elior ... I was ill ...

Do it!

And Lur was gone, leaving Zaphreth breathless and trembling.

CHAPTER 19

Runa walked with Astara through the forest, their way lit by ghostly gift-light held in the palms of two of the cloaked strangers, one tinted blue, the other green. Bran had stayed behind, no doubt to take care of the flesh traders they had left bound to a tree with ropes that glowed faintly with gift-light. Zaphreth walked behind, his steps strong and confident thanks to Astara's healing touch.

"How long have you served King Elior?" Runa asked Astara as they walked.

"I grew up in his service," Astara replied. "As soon as I could hold a bow my father taught me to shoot. And as soon as I was of age, I went out with the King's Guard to seek out flesh traders."

"You are Tree-Dwellers!" Runa exclaimed at the realisation. Astara threw a smile at Runa over her shoulder.

189

"We are."

"I thought you were just in books!"

"We are in books?" Astara laughed.

"Yes – I read about you in Prince Rael's histories! You helped him. And Lady Bruseia, the blessed."

"We did indeed. Though that was long before I was born, of course."

Runa could hardly take her eyes off Astara's back, her cloak flowing almost to the floor, yet brushing past branches and thorns without even snagging. Her pace was fast, yet she seemed to glide over the ground while Runa tripped and stumbled noisily over twigs and crunched through leaves. For Runa, it was as if she had stepped into a fairy tale. She was walking with Tree-Dwellers through the forest of Callenlas, on her way to ride a dragon to meet King Elior. Her fatigue made everything seem slightly out of time, dream-like, and a few times she shook herself to make sure she truly was awake.

They left the forest in the morning light, the Day-Star rising pale from the forest, throwing long shadows before them. The air was cold and damp but held the promise of a fine day ahead.

Runa and Zaphreth waited with Astara, shivering more from tiredness than cold, while the two men went silently in opposite directions to locate any sky riders.

After a while, Astara nodded.

"This way," she pointed south along the uneven line of the forest. "Karei has found Phaelon."

"Did he Send to you?" Runa asked, wading through the long grass, still wet with dew, though the Day-Star was already half-way to its zenith.

"Yes."

"I want to learn to Send properly," Runa said, thinking how useful it would have been when she was lost in the forest.

"You can," Astara replied, with a curious look at Runa. "You've been Sending for help for the last few days. One of our Seers heard you, and the King Sent us an urgent message as well. That was how we found you – we were posted to another area of the forest entirely."

Runa felt a little dizzy. The King had heard her? From so far away? Even more wonderful – he had answered.

"I didn't think it had got anywhere!" she exclaimed.

"Why don't you try to Send King Elior your message again?" Astara suggested, a frown of concern on her face as she paused to look at Runa. "You look very tired."

Runa shook her head. Though she had not been properly taught, she knew that the real skill in Sending lay in finding the mind of the person you needed. It was the difference between whispering in someone's ear and shouting a message out across a room. Unconsciously,

Runa fingered her uncle's jewel, hard beneath her tunic and shirt. She had to bring it to the King. It might give him further clues to the enemy's plans.

"I have no skill in it," she said. "I might Send to anyone. I can't risk it."

Astara tilted her head in acknowledgement.

They stepped off grass onto a level road of beaten earth and walking became much easier. The forest lay to their left; to their right, fields of wheat and grain spread as far as the horizon, slowly turning to gold as the Day-Star rose.

In less than an hour, Runa's dearest dream was realised. Curled asleep near the forest lay a beautiful green valley dragon, almost indistinguishable from the long grass. From its slender nose a delicate double spiral of smoke rose in the morning air, and, as Runa drew near, the dragon drew a deep breath and let it out in a sigh.

"Rider Phaelon," Astara greeted the dragon's master. "This is Runa. She has an urgent message for King Elior. Can you carry her south to the King?"

"I can," the sky rider said. "If she can keep still for many an hour and not scream or take fright easily."

Runa nodded, temporarily struck dumb with almost unbearable anticipation.

"Is she simple?" the rider whispered to Astara.

"Just excited and exhausted," Astara replied.

"How soon can we get to the King?" Runa managed to ask.

"We'll have to wait for Ragnik and his rider to carry your friend," the sky rider answered, his eyes shifting to the northern horizon. "And the wind is against us; but we should reach the camp shortly after dark."

Runa nodded with grim satisfaction. Astara spread a blanket on the damp grass so that Runa and Zaphreth could rest while they waited, and the Tree-Dwellers shared a late breakfast of nuts, dried fruit, and oatcakes with them. Runa's gaze kept drifting across to the valley dragon, whose long, purple tongue licked at her hind leg as she slept.

"Would you have told me the truth by yourself?" Zaphreth asked abruptly. "About why you needed to see King Elior?"

Runa startled guiltily and pressed her lips together.

"Yes," she said, slowly. "But you're a tSardian. I'd only just met you. I couldn't exactly tell you I knew vital war secrets, could I?"

"Got any other secrets you want to share?"

Affronted by Zaphreth's tone and feeling guilty for continuing to conceal her identity, Runa flicked a crumb of oatcake at Zaphreth and grinned.

"Not yet," she said, hoping to lighten the situation. She just was not ready to be Princess Runa again. To her relief, Zaphreth's blue eyes responded with a laugh and he flicked a crumb back at her.

Phaelon gave a shout and waved at the sky. As they all turned, shielding their eyes from the slanting rays of the Day-Star, the angular shape of a massive black dragon grew in size and clarity in the northern sky. With a rush of broad wings, and the rasp of scales, the vast form came to land, staggering to a halt in the grass just in front of them all.

"Nice landing," Phaelon complimented as the rider slipped off, removing the tight hood worn by all sky riders. A length of dark hair tumbled loose, and Runa's heart skipped a beat as the woman stepped lightly towards them.

"Thanks," she said, nodding at Phaelon. She introduced herself to the others with a flick of her long hair. "I'm Briea and this is Ragnik."

The great black gave a snort and shook his wings, sending gusts of cool air over the entire party. Runa laughed, her eyes dancing.

Astara explained the situation again for Briea's benefit, and the two riders began preparing for the long journey.

"You're smaller," Phaelon said, nodding at Runa. "So you'd better come with me."

"Rope her on," Astara cautioned the rider. "She is very tired."

Runa felt a little insulted as the rider pulled out lengths of rope, but she could not bring herself to argue.

Together, they approached the dragon and Phaelon gently coaxed her from sleep.

"Come on, girl," he whispered, gently tickling her chin. Her long mouth creased open revealing rows of gleaming white teeth as long as Runa's little finger. "Someone needs our help."

The dragon almost smiled, snuffling and puffing out clouds of steaming breath into the cool morning air. She shook her head and sat up, stretching her wings and flapping them, stirring the grass and Runa's hair. She laughed, and the dragon's purple eyes flicked around to look at her.

"This is Runa," Phaelon said. "We're going to give her a ride."

"Are you sure she will take me?" Runa asked. "The dragons in my fath– uh, in Feldemoore's fleet will only carry their own riders."

Phaelon snorted.

"Feldemoore has always lagged in dragon lore," he said. "Eralia will do as she is told, won't you, my beauty."

If Runa had not felt Phaelon's mutual admiration for the dragon, she would have found it easier to be affronted. Phaelon gave Eralia a piece of meat from his bag, which she gulped down in one swallow. Then he boosted Runa onto her back, roping her about the waist so that she could not slip off. Although the dragon, nose to tail, would easily fill a barn, she was very slender. Her breadth was similar to that of a fat donkey. And because her bones were hollow, like a bird's, she was lighter than she appeared.

Runa, barely able to breathe at being closer to a dragon than she had ever been before, stroked Eralia's scales. They looked like small green pebbles with an iridescent sheen, bubbling over her skin.

Phaelon swung himself up in front of her, taking the reins which hung from gold rings in each of Eralia's nostrils. With the lightest tug on each leather strap, he could direct her left and right. Eralia would also respond to his verbal commands, whispered gently into her ears.

With a heart-stopping jerk, Eralia spread her wings to their full breadth, each once more than twice the length of a tall man. Flapping hard, the dragon rose, the land dropping away as she gained momentum. Astara and her companions waved as they grew smaller and smaller. Moments after, Runa could hear the snort and scrape of the larger black taking off. She held Phaelon tightly as they banked and turned to the south, the fields of Callenlas spreading out around them, bathed in the Day-Star's light.

It was everything Runa had ever imagined and more.

The rhythm of the dragon's wings was slow and steady, and every now and then she would catch an updraft and simply soar. The land below looked like one of the miniature models of Feldemoore that father had in the library, studded with tiny felt trees, and toy farmhouses. The wind rushed past Runa's ears and she dared to let go of Phaelon with one hand to pull up the hood of her cloak. Phaelon wore a jacket of tan leather with a tight-fitting hood, and Runa wished she had something similar, for the wind crept through every crevice in her clothes to freeze the skin beneath. Not that she cared.

Shortly after taking off, they passed over Orr, its walls and turrets golden in the light. The capital of Callenlas was every bit as beautiful and magnificent as Runa had imagined. Two sentry dragons, both mountain blues, spotted them from a distance and flew with them as they passed over Orr. Phaelon signalled to both, and they greeted him with signs of friendship.

After a rest at noon, when Runa and Zaphreth dozed in the warmth of the Day-Star, and Eralia drank with surprising delicacy from the Telaris River, they climbed again into the air. The miles fell away beneath them, and eventually Runa's tiredness and the gentle rhythm of the flight caught up with her. She fell asleep against Phaelon's back and slept through most of the afternoon. She woke with a jerk, having slipped sideways off Phaelon's support, and bit back a yelp as the restraining ropes held her secure.

"Where are we?" she called to Phaelon, her words all but snatched away by the wind.

"The border," Phaelon shouted, pointing ahead.

The Day-Star was sinking fast in the west, bathing the whole miniature world below in a glow of orange and gold. The plains of Callenlas were giving way to the wastelands of the south, and to the southeast Runa could see the bushy greens of the forest that covered the border between Callenlas and tSardia. Immediately ahead of them, still only a smudge against the darkening horizon, lay the great desert of the south, where the battlelines were formed.

"Was it really caused by a curse?" Runa asked.

"The desert? Yes. The Lady Silendia cursed the land after the division of the kingdom to hinder tSardia in their attempts at conquering the north."

It was too difficult to talk with the muffling rush of air, and the wind stealing their words. Runa watched the sky and earth shift through hues of darkening blue until the stars began to emerge in the east. Despite being so high on the dragon's back, the stars appeared no closer, and Runa wondered just how far away they truly were.

Some nights, watching from her bedroom window, Runa had thought the stars seemed so close that she could reach out and run her fingers through them. She imagined they would tinkle like shards of crystal, but now she thought that sound too small. Perhaps they would resonate like the tubular bells played sometimes for the court's entertainment, a richer sound, rippling through the heavens, full of joy.

Lights began to appear below, small oases of yellow and orange in the expanse of shadow. Runa felt Eralia's pace shift slightly, then she banked alarmingly, and they circled downwards. Runa gripped the rider's leather coat as tightly as she could. As they slowed, Runa found she had her eyes screwed tightly shut and opened them cautiously. A long cluster of flickering lights, mirroring the scattered stars, lay spread below them in an uneven strip. She realised they were campfires and torches, and then she could see the jagged triangles of shadowy tents. Then came a jerk and the dull thud of four clawed feet against soft soil. They had landed.

Dazed and stiff, Runa allowed Phaelon to untie her and lift her down. Her legs ached from holding tightly to the dragon's sides and she could barely stand, but she refused to give in to weakness.

Zaphreth had landed first, the larger black having covered the miles more easily. He was sitting in a pale heap, clearly exhausted. He got awkwardly to his feet as Runa offered him a grin of encouragement.

"I'll have to see King Elior first," she said, "But I'm sure we can rest soon."

Zaphreth nodded mutely and Runa wondered if he had been afraid while riding Ragnik. The black was rather formidable, almost twice the size of Eralia, now tearing at a large hunk of meat with his long teeth.

Phaelon spoke to a sentry, who summoned another, and then Runa was escorted through the camp with Zaphreth, too quickly to even thank Eralia and Phaelon. They passed tents and fires with clusters of men gathered around, hulking shadows around orange flames. Some were cooking, and the smell of roasting meat or baking flatbread made Runa faint with hunger.

After a walk that felt far too long to Runa's weary legs, they reached a cluster of larger tents and the sentry stopped to address the double guard. This must be where the King and his nearest commanders stayed.

The sentry began speaking to the guards, when around the corner came a tall figure, his navy robes sweeping the dry grass and the dust. Runa's knees almost buckled as her eyes drifted up into the very last face she had expected to see.

"Uncle Izzecha!"

He stopped abruptly and looked at her with his piercing eyes. There was a heartbeat's pause, while the sentry and the guards failed to notice the minute interaction between Izzecha and Runa.

Then, without missing a beat, Uncle Izzecha rushed forward and swept Runa into his arms.

"Runa!" he exclaimed. "My dear Runa! Where have you been?"

Runa stiffened under his embrace. She noticed that his blue stone had been replaced with a glimmering violet one; it dangled near her nose as he held her at arm's length, seemingly looking at her in glad amazement. Unnoticed, the fingers of his left hand turned the violet jewel slightly from side to side.

Runa felt herself to be in intense danger. But tiredness created a kind of fog in her brain and her thoughts drifted like thick mist.

"My niece," Izzecha was proclaiming to the guards. "My niece – the one everyone has been searching for. You must allow me to take her to King Mabrigas, he has been worried sick."

"I have orders to take her to King Elior." The sentry wavered, but Izzecha dismissed him with a wave of his hand.

"Would you keep a child from her father when he has been seeking her for days? Look at her – she is half-starved and exhausted, no doubt sick. She is in no fit state to be presented to King Elior. Let me take her to her father where she can be cared for. Tomorrow she can be presented to the King."

"I was told it was urgent ..." The sentry appeared concerned, but Uncle Izzecha fingered his purple stone, while his right hand remained firmly on Runa's shoulder. The sentry shook his head and stepped back, relinquishing Runa.

"No ..." Runa murmured, but the weariness that she had been fighting all day lay over her like a thick blanket. Though she knew she ought to be going in the other direction, running, she could not break free of Uncle Izzecha. Her feet could barely lift to pace over the ground; she felt herself to be falling asleep while walking. She felt a foggy sense of concern for Zaphreth, who hovered behind, unnoticed by her uncle, but could not make any words come out of her mouth. Her tongue seemed to have turned to sand.

Then she was passing through the flaps of a tent into darkness; Uncle Izzecha lit his palm and dropped the jewel. The sense of foggy weariness dissipated, though Runa remained confused and unsteady.

Uncle Izzecha's face had hardened, his eyes glinting like steel, his mouth twisted with barely restrained rage and bitterness.

"And now," he said, looking at Runa. "What am I to do with you?"

Runa stepped back and brushed against the soft inner

fabric of the tent. It was a small space, furnished with only a table of rough wood and a sleeping mat. Uncle Izzecha's blue light did not provide much illumination. Her wits were slowly returning. Uncle Izzecha's violet stone must have had something to do with her brain-fog, she realised ... could she duck around him and escape the tent?

"To think that a kid could cause me so much trouble," Izzecha was muttering, while continuing to stare at her. Runa could not imagine what was running through his mind, but she felt the danger in his eyes like a fist around her throat.

Not taking his eyes off her, Izzecha moved to a small lamp hanging from the central pole of the tent and lit it.

It was a small chance, but Runa took it, diving for the entrance, opening her mouth to yell loudly.

"Help!" she managed to squeak, before Uncle Izzecha's arms were about her, and she felt the unmistakeably cool pressure of a blade at her throat.

"A little uncouth, I'll admit," Izzecha was hissing in her ear. "But I have no qualms at all about dispatching you this way. It will make things more difficult for me, admittedly. But at least you will be out of the way and making no more trouble."

Runa felt hot tears pricking at her eyes. She was not afraid, though she knew she should be. She was crying because she had tried so hard and done so much, and it was all to be for nothing. Izzecha would win, tSardia would be helped, and that was unbearable to her. Evil should never win.

Evil would not win. If she was to die, she would go down fighting.

She could feel the hilt of her dagger, her mother's paper knife, under her fingers.

Then Zaphreth burst through the door of the tent, his eyes widening as he took in Runa's situation.

Runa bit down on her uncle's fingers as hard as she could, until her mouth filled with blood and he yelled with pain. In the same moment her fingers gripped the dagger and she wrested it upwards out of its sheath. As Izzecha's grip on her loosened momentarily, she drove the dagger back into his side. The sensation of flesh giving way to blade was sickening but Izzecha released her, groaning. His own knife fell to the floor.

Izzecha gave another cry as Zaphreth threw out bright blue ropes of light, pinning the man's upper arms to his torso so that he was forced to release Runa.

"How dare you attack me!" Izzecha raged, in the same breath hurling out an ugly, unfamiliar word. A blast of light filled the tent, shattering Zaphreth's power. To Runa's horror, her friend crumpled to the floor.

"Here! To me!" Runa shouted, darting forward to

snatch the dagger up. Izzecha's face was snarling in rage, and he drew back his hand, gathering power to hurl at her.

Runa ducked, and the tent burst open, a hoard of armed men entering.

"Seize him!" Runa meant to exclaim. "He is a traitor."

What actually came out of her mouth (in a very un-riderly squeak) was, "Traitor!"

"Ware, magic!" one guard shouted, and before Izzecha could do another thing, a Master stepped forward and threw out bands of power. Glowing yellow ropes twined about Izzecha and held him fast. They prevented him from casting any spells or using any magic.

The veins in Izzecha's neck bulged and his face turned the colour of a tomato, but he was helpless, pinioned in the powerful hold of the Master who would not take his eyes off the prisoner.

"Who are you, maiden?" one of the guards asked, helping her to her feet.

"The Princess Runa of Feldemoore," she replied, for now Izzecha was taken there was no more need for pretence.

The tent door opened once more, and into the now crowded space stepped none other than King Mabrigas.

"Runa!" he exclaimed, his face as shocked as it had ever been. "What are you doing here? And why is my brother bound?"

CHAPTER 20

It took some time to sort out the confusion in the small tent. Runa had to explain very quickly about her uncle's part in her disappearance, and all the while her concern for Zaphreth was growing. He lay very still, clearly damaged by her uncle's magic.

"Please, father," Runa said at last, interrupting King Mabrigas's tirade of questions. "Uncle Izzecha attacked my friend."

Healers were sent for and Zaphreth was carefully carried to their tents. Izzecha was also taken away in bonds, ranting angrily about princesses who should know their place and stay there. Runa's weariness finally overcame her, and she sank onto the floor while the tent slowly cleared.

At last, King Mabrigas seemed to notice her fatigue.

"I'm sorry, father," Runa said, remembering suddenly

that Uncle Izzecha was her father's brother. She had been brave for so long, and now with her father looking so sad and so worried, she suddenly found herself giving in to her feelings. Tears ran hot down her cheeks, and she choked on sobs. The betrayal of her uncle, the fear of his apprehending her in the forest, all the emotions she had fought during her long journey rose up like the waves of the sea.

"You mustn't be sorry," her father pulled her up into his arms and his dark beard was rough against her cheek. He smelled of cedar oil and rosemary, familiar and masculine. The silk of his robe was soft, and Runa leaned into his warm strength.

"I brought the weapon," Runa remembered, fumbling with her tunic and shirt with shaking hands.

"What weapon?"

"The weapon Uncle Izzecha was going to use."

Runa drew out the jewel, its sapphire depths glinting in the light.

Father peered keenly at it, raising his hand to touch it.

"Careful —" Runa tried to warn him, but he made contact before she spoke and drew a sharp breath inward as the magic tingled against his fingertip.

"I must see King Elior," Runa added.

"You must eat first," her father insisted, steering Runa out of the small tent and through the camp, to a much larger tent, furnished and lit with several lanterns. A servant brought a tray of food while King Mabrigas fussed about, pouring Runa a drink of spiced wine and raking the brazier, though it was far from cold. In all her life Runa had never seen him serve anyone and she could not at first bring herself to take the cup from his hand, but the tray was loaded with soft bread and cold chicken, sweet cheese and glistening slices of orange and apple. Runa realised she was thirsty and ravenous.

"I must see King Elior," she repeated through a mouthful of chicken, bread and butter.

"What is so urgent?"

"When Uncle Izzecha kidnapped me," Runa replied, swallowing with a gulp. "I overheard him talking to a tSardian lord about a weapon so powerful you would not dare to join King Elior in the war."

Father frowned; his dark eyes puzzled.

"I thought it must be this," Runa said, glancing at the jewel, now lying on the table. "I must tell the King. I cannot trust anyone else. Not after Uncle Izzecha."

"The King is no doubt asleep," father said gently. "And your uncle was too late. I have already given King Elior my support – it is why I am here, with our fleet, and our army is on the way by ship."

A sluice of disappointment at not having a reason to meet King Elior dampened Runa's relief that her father had done the right thing.

Then the tent door flapped open, admitting a sigh of night air. The two servers dropped to their knees and King Mabrigas stood.

In the doorway, framed by a navy sky studded with crystal stars, stood King Elior. His cloak of war shifted in shades of crimson and deep red. The lamplight turned his hair and beard to a river of gold, and his blue eyes flashed like sapphires. His posture and energy suggested youth and vigour; but when Runa dared to look into his eyes she found them old - no, ageless, brimming with wisdom and truth and light. It was like looking into the heart of a star.

As soon as she realised who he was, she knelt. Her heart pounded, and her mouth was dry. For the first time in her life, she wished she had brushed her hair and washed, and was wearing a nice dress. For him it would be worth it. He was a presence more powerful than she had ever imagined in reading the stories in her father's library; and yet, when he spoke there was a warmth and an intimacy that surprised her and made her heart ache with longing.

The kings exchanged courtly greetings and Runa was pleased to hear her father honouring King Elior as the greater king. Then his hand was extended to raise her and King Elior spoke to her in that warm, deep voice that

Runa felt could awaken the very earth beneath her feet, and at the same time resonate across the heavens like music.

"Your father has been turning whole kingdoms upside down in search of you."

"I'm sorry, my King," Runa answered, her voice trembling a little. "I didn't mean to cause trouble."

"It wasn't your fault, Runa," father said.

"But it was my fault, father," Runa answered, her cheeks burning crimson. She found, in the presence of the King, that she could not help but tell the truth, even though it shamed her. "I ran away. If I hadn't, Uncle Izzecha wouldn't have been able to take me."

"We'll say no more of that for the present," King Elior said. "I understand you have an urgent message for me."

"My uncle, on the ship he spoke about a weapon he intended to use that would dissuade father from joining you in the war," Runa blurted, the relief of finally unburdening herself making her forget for a moment who she was speaking to. Words rushed out of her like a flood. "I tried my best, Sir – I threw all his magic overboard, and when we were shipwrecked I stole his jewel, thinking it might be the weapon. I tried to reach you sooner, but I was captured by fleshtraders and held up. As soon as the Tree-Dwellers rescued me I flew here on a dragon. Uncle Izzecha is now bound and unable to work magic, but I do not know if he managed to make another weapon and deliver it to tSardia already."

Runa hung her head, suddenly exhausted, missing the glances of astonished admiration that passed between her father and the King.

"May I see the jewel?"

King Mabrigas held it out to Elior by its chain.

King Elior moved across the tent with the jewel and took a seat. Mabrigas also sat, and Runa took the tapestried footstool.

King Elior examined the jewel for some time. He seemed untroubled by touching it, and even tested it momentarily, making it produce a strange, vibrating glow.

"It is magic, and certainly powerful," he pronounced at last. "But I do not see how it would be a weapon of any magnitude."

Runa felt herself sinking with disappointment. She had failed.

"What were his words exactly," King Elior asked, folding the chain about the jewel and secreting it in his robes.

"He said ..." Runa sighed, then shook her head impatiently. "I can't remember."

"Try," the King said gently. He smiled as he spoke, his eyes looking right into Runa's, and somehow, she found she had the strength. She took a deep breath and closed her eyes, recalling the moment on the ship. It felt like months ago, not days, and took a great effort, wading back through events which had been so full of fear and difficulty. There were so many things crowding her head.

"He was talking to Lord Swarlor, a tSardian. He said that his brother wouldn't use force against him now because he had a weapon ..."

Runa closed her eyes and dragged herself back to the ship. She could feel the deck warm and smooth beneath her hands, the slow rising and falling of the ship passing through the waves. She could hear her uncle's voice.

"He said, 'now we have a weapon in our hands that could turn the whole outcome of the war.'"

There was a long pause while the two kings considered her words.

"Could it be that he was speaking figuratively?" King Elior said at length. "Could it be that it is not a literal weapon, rather that he meant something which would work as a weapon by affecting the war?"

King Mabrigas shifted to be more upright.

"Runa, I think your uncle meant you," King Elior said finally, with a smile.

"Me?" Runa retorted, and then realised that her tone was rude. "I mean, me, my King?"

"I think your uncle intended to deliver you to King

Lakesh of tSardia, so that you could be used as leverage to bribe your father. They could threaten to kill or harm you, or offer to release you, if your father remained out of the war, or even offered them military support."

Runa felt both immensely small and horribly significant at the same time.

"You wouldn't have, father, would you?" she asked in an appalled whisper. "You wouldn't have given up the country just for me?"

Runa's father was gravely silent.

"I wouldn't have known what to do, Runa," he replied. "It would have been the hardest decision of my life."

"You couldn't back down just for me!" Runa exclaimed. "tSardia can't be allowed to win!"

King Mabrigas looked at Runa with an indescribable expression and King Elior chuckled admiringly.

"Princess Runa," he said, in that rich, warm voice. "I wish my trained riders were half as brave as you! You can join my army any time you wish!"

King Mabrigas groaned, but Runa sat forward eagerly.

"Do you mean it?" she exclaimed. "I have always wanted to be a sky rider!"

King Elior laughed again, and Runa's father shook his head.

"Now then, before I leave and get some sleep, is there anything else you learned from Izzecha, any names, any knowledge of the enemy that I should know?"

Runa shook her head.

"I don't think so. He said something about a Lord Lur, but that's all I can remember."

"Lord Lur?" King Elior's face whitened, and he sank back, stunned. "You are certain, absolutely certain that was the name you heard?"

"I ... I think so," Runa felt suddenly anxious now she was on the spot. "Yes. Lur. I think – I'm sure."

"Lur ..." Elior whispered. His fingers curled about his hilt instinctively, his eyes distant and full of dread.

"I thought the demon was banished, Lord?" King Mabrigas said.

King Elior did not reply.

"I must go," he said. "I must summon my council. This war is bigger than we knew."

Runa and her father bowed as the King left. Then King Mabrigas turned to her, his dark eyes seeking hers.

"Runa," he said. "There is so much I must say to you, and I cannot stay long. But first ... I am sorry. Since you went missing, I realised how little I have had to do with you over the years. I thought ... I thought that I would not be able to replace the mother you lost, and that I could not be a parent to you. I put my kingdom first. I am sorry. I was wrong. I should have been more of a father to you, not less, to make up for your lack. Please will you forgive me."

Runa's throat tightened and her heart burned in her chest. She had expected to be in such trouble; had a formal apology all prepared. And now her father was sorry.

"I do," she said, twisting her mouth. "And I'm sorry too. I shouldn't have run away. I should have attended my lessons."

King Mabrigas placed his hand on the back of her head and gave her a warm smile.

"Now, you need sleep, and –" King Mabrigas sniffed. "A bath. And I am afraid I must join the council."

Runa recognised the gravity of the situation. She had a vague memory of reading of the banishing of Lur in the histories ... but hadn't he been a beast? A monster?

Father left, with a final backward glance, and then two female servers appeared and took Runa to another tent where there was a basin of hot water to wash in, and a clean nightgown. Her hair was washed but proved so matted and tangled that they had to cut it. The one server held up a polished brass mirror for Runa to examine her new appearance, her face apologetic.

"I'm sorry, my Lady, but we had to cut it so short ..."

She stopped as Runa found herself in the mirror and stared at the stranger who met her there. Gone was the long, straight hair of an awkward girl. Now her green eyes looked out from a frame of curving, copper fronds that just skimmed her jaw.

"It's perfect!" she said to the server's evident relief.

ဆ * ର

The kings remained in council through the night and were still in conference when Runa finally woke at almost noon the next day. She ate a meal and discovered that fried bacon and eggs when you are starving, is the best taste in the whole world. With her father occupied, Runa went in search of Zaphreth.

Her first thought upon rising had been to ask after her friend, but the servers who brought her breakfast knew nothing about Zaphreth. Once Runa had eaten, they directed her to the healers' tents, near the back of the camp.

Runa strode between the tents, still wearing the dress and boots her uncle had given her, ages ago it seemed now, in Faradel. The sea had washed some of the colour out of the fabric, and there were a few small tears in the dress, but in a camp of war there was no hope of finding any clothes for a girl of thirteen. Runa did not mind; she still liked the dress which was far more practical than any of the dresses she had ever owned before, even though it reminded her of Uncle Izzecha.

Zaphreth was still sleeping when she found the right tent, though the healer looking after him said he would soon feel better.

"He woke up last night," the healer explained to Runa, "and took some food. He had some burns to his hands, but nothing too serious. He just needs rest."

When Runa peered around the healer, hoping to get a glimpse of the tSardian, the healer stood stubbornly in the way. In the end, Runa took the hint and wandered along the northern edge of the camp to where the dragons were kept when not on duty. She had hoped to see Eralia and Phaelon, but the beautiful green dragon was nowhere to be seen. Instead, a fire dragon was tearing at a hunk of meat and, curled up behind it like a gigantic cat, slept a mountain blue.

Runa crept as close as she dared. The blue was small, probably only just fledged, and its wings were almost purple at the tips, while its other scales glimmered with iridescence. As Runa crouched to watch it sleep, its large eyelids flickered, and its great head turned slowly to look at Runa. Its eyes were bright green with purple flecks in them, the pupil reduced to a vertical slit in the glare of the noon light.

Runa froze; she was still ten paces away but that was nothing to an irritated blue. The dragon stared at her for such a long time Runa wondered if perhaps it could not see her. Then it blew a jet of steam from its nostrils and turned its head to nose at an itch on its hindleg. Runa felt a little insulted at being deemed so insignificant, but cautiously backed away before finding somewhere safer to sit. She watched the dragons through the long afternoon, enjoying the warmth of the Day-Star and the pleasure of resting after such a long and difficult journey.

She wondered who Lord Lur was. Could he be the monster Prince Rael had faced? Runa could not remember much of the story. It was two hundred years old and blended into all the other legends she had read. Whoever Lord Lur was, he had clearly troubled King Elior.

She wondered when she could return to Zaphreth's tent. Perhaps she could wait for the healer to be distracted and sneak in to see her friend. In the meantime, Runa plucked a stem of grass and worked at holding it in the air, as Zaphreth had taught her in the hut. It never hurt to practise.

CHAPTER 21

In fact, Zaphreth had just woken and was feeling, for once, like the prince he claimed to be. The mattress he lay on was soft, and he had two feather pillows to rest against. A female healer entered, bearing a tray of food.

"You're in a state, aren't you?" she muttered, feeling his head as Ama would have, making him feel homesick. She fed him as much porridge as he could take, salted and sweetened with honey, and brought a plate of apples and pears for him to eat as he pleased. She gave him a small cup of bitter medicine, and then left him to sleep again.

Zaphreth lay back in the bed, determined to enjoy this experience. He had not eaten his fill since the tavern on the border, and he had never slept on anything so soft and comfortable. There was also a curious, unexpected peace lying deep inside his chest. It was somehow connected to the way he had leaped to Runa's defence the previous evening.

Exhausted and faintly nauseous from the long dragon ride, he had followed Runa through the camp in a daze, longing just for a mat to sleep on, and perhaps some food. When the well-dressed man greeted Runa, Zaphreth had simply observed, accustomed to being ignored. Only as the man steered Runa away from the guards did something in Zaphreth stir, a suspicion that the man was leading Runa a bit too insistently.

When the man and Runa entered the little tent, Zaphreth had hovered outside, cursing his own hesitancy. He was anxious that Runa would forget him, and he would lose his opportunity to be introduced to King Elior. The cool night air was beginning to refresh him a little, and he could hear the man's voice low inside the tent. Something was wrong, he was sure, but lacked the confidence to intervene.

Then Runa shouted for help and all Zaphreth's uncertainty disappeared. In fact, thought abandoned him, and he acted entirely on instinct. Bursting into the tent, it had taken one glance at Runa's frightened eyes and the grip the strange man had on her for him to raise his hand and throw bonds of Mind Power around the assailant. Only after did he consider that throwing blind force would have injured Runa as well as her uncle. It was strange, this remembered sense of his own bravery, but in a pleasant way, like the stiffness of new clothing.

The feelings he had towards Runa were less comfortable. Though he liked the sense of companionship she woke in him, the protectiveness was more of a problem. She was his enemy, he had to remind himself firmly, on the side of King Elior. He had tried to probe her the day before, to see if she would tell him her information, but she had frustratingly deflected the question.

Zaphreth's fingers unconsciously traced the scar in his palm. He had to Send something to Lur. No doubt Runa had reported her message to King Elior already, which was unfortunate. Perhaps he could find her and get her to introduce him to the King now, though the thought made him tremble. It had been tricky enough lying to Bran, with the darkness to help his deceit. Zaphreth had strong doubts that he could lie so easily to the King of Callenlas, who was clearly skilled in trickery himself, to maintain such a hold over people like Runa.

Though he would have loved to stay in bed for the rest of the day, Zaphreth made himself get up. He found a basin of warm water on a table and some clean clothes – a pair of brown trousers and a light shirt. There was no tunic, but the air this far south was very warm. Zaphreth washed and dressed, taking an apple from the bowl before slipping out of the tent. He half-expected a healer to stop him and send him back to bed, but the area near his tent was quiet.

Zaphreth wondered where Runa was. His eyes had been tightly shut as the dragon descended over the camp yesterday, but he guessed the tents sprawled quite far along the border. Still, she could not be too far away. Zaphreth decided to search for her with his mind, cautiously, for he still felt weakened by Izzecha's attack.

Runa's presence was surprisingly close, a green cloud of intensity near enough to be only a few paces away. Zaphreth blinked in surprise and stepped around the next tent, to find Runa running towards him across the grass, a big grin on her face. Were it not for her hair, burnished brighter than ever by the afternoon Day-Star, he would hardly have recognised her (and even her hair was different, cut so that it skimmed her jaw, making her appear older). She wore her ankle-length tunic of soft amber fabric, freshly cleaned, but with a gold chain about her waist for a belt, and a circlet of gold about her head. Zaphreth felt a wave of intimidation; had she not come running up like a gangly colt he would not have known how to address her.

"I'm so glad you're up!"

Runa threw her arms about him, catching him by surprise. Zaphreth hugged her back bashfully, still puzzled by her fine belt and the gold circlet. In his experience, even wealthy merchants' daughters did not wear gold coronets. Perhaps Feldemoore had different customs, though he had his doubts.

"You look a bit different," she said, suddenly shy, taking in Zaphreth's clean hair and clothes.

"Anything's better than a dress," he said, tugging at his tunic.

"Much better," Runa grinned. "And you look much better. Well, even."

Zaphreth did not know what to say. He realised that he owed his recovery, at least in part to her care in the hut, but could not bring himself to thank her; it felt awkward, and she was such an ardent devotee of King Elior.

"Look—" Runa's eyes held an expectant glint as she picked a stem of grass and held it out in her palm. Zaphreth could see the concentration in her face as the stem fluttered in her palm and then rose, to hover in the air for a wobbly moment. With a gasp of effort, Runa let it fall, and it spun to the ground. "I've been practising," she told him, clearly expecting him to be impressed.

"It's good," Zaphreth said, surprised at his sincerity and the glow of pride that he had successfully imparted knowledge to someone else.

"Come on, you must meet father," Runa said. "He only just got back to his tent."

Runa dragged him towards the camp and waved at the sentry as they passed between the first tents.

"Princess," the sentry greeted Runa with a friendly grin.

"I've been waiting here for you all afternoon," Runa said. "Marrus there kept me company."

"Princess ...?" Zaphreth wondered aloud, gaping at the sentry as they passed. "What?"

But he did not get any further. In a blinding flash Lur's presence entered his mind, rocking him to his knees so that Runa let go of his hand.

What is happening? Lur demanded, his presence blazing. *What is happening in the camp?*

I just woke up ... Zaphreth Sent desperately, realising with panic that the General had no idea that he had been attacked. *Give me time.*

Thankfully Lur released him, and Zaphreth crouched, trying to regain his composure.

"Are you alright?" Runa asked, bending over him anxiously. "What happened?"

"I'm not sure," Zaphreth shook his head and made himself stand. "Must still be dizzy from the magic."

Runa watched him.

"You're still not well," she said. "Come and have something to eat. You can eat with father."

"Who is your father?" Zaphreth asked, still dazed by Lur's sudden intrusion, and Runa being addressed as royalty.

"Umm," she looked away, still urging a fast pace despite her concern about Zaphreth. She seemed not to want to answer, and her reply was spoken quickly in a low tone. "King Mabrigas of Feldemoore," she muttered.

"What?" Zaphreth almost fell over a second time. "You're a princess? An actual princess?"

"So?" Runa mumbled.

"So ...! Shouldn't I have been calling you 'Your Highness' or 'Princess Runa' all this time? I probably shouldn't be talking to you at all."

"Why not? You're a noble. And I don't care about things like that anyway." Runa pulled a face. "I've never wanted to be a princess. It was nice, just being known as myself for a while. Didn't you like that? Just being Zaphreth for a while? Instead of 'Prince Zaphreth' or 'Sir Zaphreth' or whatever you go by. I've been so lonely."

'Oh yes, it must be very lonely to live in a palace surrounded by servants and courtiers,' was the reply that Zaphreth only just bit back in time. Instead, he stared at Runa for a long time. He had never considered that being royal, or rich, would come with troubles. He had only ever seen the privilege, the comforts.

"Come on," Princess Runa urged again, and they pressed on through the tents.

Their forced pace through the camp was interrupted

several times by Lur's demands: *What is happening?* They lacked the initial force of the first Sending, and Zaphreth managed to hold himself together, stumbling only a little each time, so Runa barely noticed. As they came nearer to the centre of the camp, where the kings' and generals' tents were, both children became aware that something momentous was occurring. Runa, waiting at the back of the camp for Zaphreth's arrival, had heard the horns sounding instructions to the army on the field, a good mile and a half south of the camp. But she had little understanding of what the different calls meant.

Here, at the centre of the camp, soldiers and squires ran about with messages, armfuls of weapons, folded flags and banners, and supplies. Dull but insistent in the background was the thud of a thousand marching feet and a drum keeping time.

"What's going on?" Runa asked a squire as he hurried past.

"The King sounded a general retreat!" he replied, his eyes bulging with the effort of bearing three shields piled on top of each other. He hurried on, and Runa turned to Zaphreth with a mystified look in her eyes. But Zaphreth had even less knowledge than Runa.

As Runa looked for her father, Zaphreth crouched and pretended to be removing a stone from his shoe. While he did so, he managed to draw enough strength to Send briefly to Lur.

Army in retreat.

Within a few heartbeats, the warlord thundered back into Zaphreth's mind, *I know that! Why?!*

I'll find out, Zaphreth answered, hoping that he could.

"He's here!" Runa beckoned to Zaphreth from a tent doorway. Zaphreth hurried to her side and was drawn inside the large tent. He found it simply furnished, with a polished wood table and two chairs in the centre, a low bed with a coverlet embroidered with the Feldemoorian crest, and a small brazier, currently unlit.

In one of the chairs sat a man of average height with dark curling hair and beard, scribbling away busily at some parchments scattered on the table. He smiled warmly, his dark eyes friendly. If it were not for his fine robes and Runa's introduction, Zaphreth would not have guessed he was a king. He did not even wear a circlet to indicate his title.

"King Mabrigas," Runa said, with a roguish twinkle in her eyes. "May I present Lord Zaphreth of ... sorry, I forgot your title. Of tSardia, anyway. Zaphreth, this is my father."

Zaphreth executed an awkward bow, scraping his hurried lessons in etiquette from his memory.

"Lord Zaphreth of Talivera," he said, trembling inside.

King Mabrigas gestured to the second chair with a

welcoming smile. Runa produced a small canvas stool which folded out, for herself to sit on.

"So, Zaphreth, you have been having some adventures," the king said, with a kind smile. "Runa has been telling me all about you."

Zaphreth felt unnerved by his unquestioning acceptance. He had expected a lengthy interrogation, possibly even torture, to determine his truthfulness.

"Yes, Sir," he replied, then blushed as he remembered that 'my King' was the correct mode of address. "My King," he added quickly.

"I understand you wish to pledge allegiance to King Elior?"

"Yes, my King," Zaphreth replied.

A squire entered, bearing a silver tray loaded with fruit, cheese, and bread. He set it down on the table, then returned a moment later with a second tray of sweetened wine in silver cups.

"With thanks to the Day-Star," King Mabrigas said, lifting a single piece of bread towards the sky. Runa did the same, so Zaphreth copied, feeling stiff and awkward.

"I am sure you have gathered that there is trouble in the camp. Once things have settled down, the King will meet with you, and you may plead your cause with him. I am quite sure he will be accommodating. He is always very kind to deserters and prisoners alike."

Zaphreth swallowed hard on the bread in his mouth. The feelings flooding him were difficult to process, at odds with everything he had been raised to believe about the north of their island. And throughout it all he was waiting tensely from the next demand from Lur for information.

"You have been through a lot," Mabrigas said gently. "It takes a great deal for a man to forsake his country and his people.

"I think at first you must go to Orr. Although you reject your people and their war, you are still of tSardian blood, legally an enemy. There will be some paperwork, I would imagine, and you would have to forsake your oath to King Lakesh first, before you could pledge to any other Lord."

"My pledge was to the General," Zaphreth said, curling his fingers over the scar in his palm. "I was pledged with blood."

"That does make things a bit more complicated," King Mabrigas said, a grave note in his voice. "But King Elior will make a way, never you fear. And first, there is the matter of the war to deal with."

"Why did the King sound the retreat?" Runa asked.

King Mabrigas drew a breath and glanced at Zaphreth.

"Father, he is my friend," Runa said. "You cannot doubt him. He has come all this way! He defended me against

Uncle Izzecha."

Still the king hesitated and Zaphreth almost wanted him to listen to his instinct and not trust him. He wanted to tell Lur he had no news, nothing to say. The urgency of this feeling surprised him. But King Mabrigas smiled at his daughter, and then at Zaphreth.

"Forgive me, Zaphreth," he said. "I did not mean to doubt your truthfulness. The King of Callenlas has called a halt to the war for the time being, now that he knows who is truly behind it."

"Behind it?" Zaphreth asked.

"Lur," Mabrigas replied. "Until now, we thought King Lakesh was driving the war, simply wanting to extend his territory into the north. Elior did not know Lur was present in tSardia."

Zaphreth's heart thudded, and he pressed his fingertips together, desperate to maintain an air of nonchalance. How did they know about Lord Lur? How did they dare to speak his name?

"Who is Lur?" Runa asked.

King Mabrigas's face clouded over, and his voice became heavy with concern. "Lur is a darkened star," he explained. "But he has a heart like a human, for he craves power and honour and glory, and cares only for himself.

"Before this world began, he led a revolt in the Fields of Light, seeking to overthrow Elior and claim power and position for himself. His place in the Council of Light was blotted out, his star darkened, and he was cast from his position. Since then, his bitterness and rage have grown, nursed inside his resentful heart. He continually seeks to conquer Elior, but if he cannot have that then he does all in his power to undo any good he finds, or to warp what is straight and true.

"Seeing that Elior was gaining power and honour among men, the dark star wanted only to end his rule on earth and establish his own kingdom. And so, he began to corrupt the hearts of some in Callenlas, promising them glory and power if they would only do his will.

"Lur was behind the division of our island into four kingdoms, during the reign of Prince Arthen. Lur incited the great war between tSardia and Callenlas during the reign of Prince Rael, when King Elior finally returned to our island. He is behind the whispers that Elior is no star, behind the lies that the stars are mere lights and have nothing to do with our lives or our destinies. He is behind the throne of tSardia, and now, we have realised, he is behind this current war."

Zaphreth licked his lips with a drying tongue. Incredulous as the words of the king were to his tSardian ears, they rang true. The two distinct feelings warred within him, as fierce as the battles that had raged on the plain to the south. The stars were lights in the sky. How

231

could they have souls? How could they appear human? How could Lur possibly be a star? It was surely nonsense.

"We were told the wars were just," Zaphreth said, being careful with his words, restraining his inner turmoil. "That when the island divided, it was because Prince Arthen chose a younger son over tSardin, the rightful heir."

"That much is true, in a way," King Mabrigas replied. "But the truth of it has been twisted until it is beyond recognition. Prince tSardin had a heart like Lur, proud and selfish. His father saw how the boy handled the small amount of power that had been entrusted to him in youth and perceived that his son would be an evil king, reigning selfishly, in the ways of Lur. His younger brother was not like him. He loved Elior and loved Callenlas. He would rule in love, with mercy and justice, the way all good princes should.

"Arthen gave tSardin many warnings and many opportunities to change. But as the boy reached manhood, he only became darker in his ways. Some think he even spoke to Lur secretly.

"When Ilfian succeeded to the throne, tSardin went to war with him. When he lost, he retreated to the south and established a new kingdom, which came to be known as tSardia.

"Ever since, the two nations have lived in an uneasy

truce, with war occasionally breaking out. This is the greatest war since the first battle that divided our island. To discover that Lur is behind it is, well, not entirely a surprise, though none of us had guessed it until now."

Zaphreth sat silently, digesting this new way of looking at history with an uneasy mind. It still seemed wrong, that the older brother should be passed over.

"Forgive me," he said quietly. "I'm still learning, but ... wasn't it the older brother's right to inherit the crown?"

He waited for Mabrigas to get angry and tell him not to question his elders, especially not the version of history they believed in so much. But the king simply nodded thoughtfully.

"With any normal crown, yes," Mabrigas replied. "The eldest child is heir by right. However, the crown of Callenlas sits on King Elior's head. The princes and princesses rule only as his representatives. They are ambassadors, not kings, there to rule by Elior's system of law and justice, not their own. A prince who rules selfishly is no prince at all and has misunderstood his role."

Neither Mabrigas nor Runa had any idea of the desperate internal battle these words began in Zaphreth's mind and heart. His reason could see the wisdom and rightness of the way Callenlas was governed. But his upbringing, and a rather loud and angry voice in his heart kept saying, *but why? Why should Elior rule? He's a star, if he is a star ... what has this world got to do with him?*

He could feel his mind clutching desperately at the words he always heard in his father's voice in his head: that the legends of the stars were a human invention, the story of Elior a hollow scaffolding for a false claim to power ...

A horn sounded nearby, and King Mabrigas rose from the chair.

"Forgive me, Lord Zaphreth; I must go," he said. "Now, this is a very dangerous place for two young people to be. I have arranged escorts for you both first thing in the morning; Runa, you will be flying north, to Lorandia."

"Oh, but father–" Runa complained loudly.

"Enough, Runa. I have no time to argue. A young girl – or boy – has no place at a battle.

"Zaphreth, an assistant of mine will be taking you to Orr, on foot, I'm afraid, as no horses can be spared. But you will be well cared for there. And once the war is over, King Elior will deal mercifully with you, I am sure."

"But, Sir, what if Lord Lur wins?" Zaphreth asked.

Runa stared at him with surprise.

"King Elior always wins," she said, a trace of scorn in her voice.

"Lord Lur is very powerful," he said doubtfully.

"You haven't met King Elior," Runa probably did not

mean to sound condescending, but she did. "When you do, you'll understand."

Zaphreth hid his inner scorn at her words, and rose to kiss King Mabrigas's hand and bow, remembering his manners.

છ૭ * ૭જ

Zaphreth lay as still as he could in the tent where King Mabrigas's servants had found him a pallet, but what he really wanted to do was pace, or run, or somehow express his inner agitation.

He felt miserable and elated at the same time. Runa was so trusting of him, so including. He had never felt so welcomed and wanted. And she was a princess! In fact, everyone was kind and trusting, from the King down to the servants. Everything he knew about the north, or thought he knew, was being challenged. Runa's faith in King Elior was irritating, and at the same time drew at him forcefully.

But Elior's claim to power remained tenuous at best. Zaphreth wondered how he would get out of being sent to Orr, or whether he could ask to meet Elior early in the morning. He was not sure how he would handle the meeting, though he had been thinking about it ever since he left Lur's camp. How would he disguise the anger and bitterness he felt towards this pretend king, this one who had ruined his homeland and torn his family apart?

A finger of terror slipped coldly into his heart as he wondered what Elior would do should he discover Zaphreth's true motives. What if Elior was like Lur, and had such power to See into souls? Zaphreth screwed his eyes up tightly. He would have to be brave. His oath to Lur burned in his palm, reminding him of all that he owed to his master, and all that he would get in return for good service.

What would Lur do with the information Zaphreth now had? Zaphreth knew his duty, knew that he could change the war by Sending his information to Lur. A week ago, he would have had no hesitation. He could not quite explain his inner doubts. Perhaps it was to do with Runa and her father, both so kind. What would happen to them if Lur attacked the camp? What would happen to Zaphreth if he waited until Runa was safely away? What if her father was killed?

Zaphreth clenched his fists. *Get hold of yourself*, he thought sternly. He thought of Ama, alone and sad in the little house by the road to Sarreia. He thought of Irek, locked away until the end of the war. He thought of the desert, slowly creeping south, eating up the fields and vineyards. Would Elior allow it to continue until nothing remained of his homeland?

He thought of the honour that would be his, after the war, when all the miserable details of prisoners and burials were over. He would be recognised as the boy who entered enemy territory and spied on a King. He would be hailed as the hero who brought an end to the oppression of Elior. He would have a palace, a soft bed, food, and a home for Ama and his father, as Lord of Talivera.

Well? What is happening?

Lur's interruption was like a searing pain running through his spine. Zaphreth gathered his strength and Sent south, finding Lur's mind easily.

Elior is in council. He knows you are the cause of war. Expect action.

He was not sure what else to say. He half-expected another blinding demand for information, but the warlord ignored him for the rest of the night.

CHAPTER 22

"Attack! Attack!"

The alarm sounded throughout the camp, joined by the sound of men fumbling to put on armour, spears clattering, shouted orders and the screams of frightened horses. The thunder of the approaching army sent a thrill of fear through Zaphreth.

The other pallets in his tent were empty, hastily evacuated, blankets disordered, even a pair of shoes left behind. Zaphreth rolled to a sitting position and forced himself to his feet. The sounds of conflict were coming closer and closer.

Outside, the camp was in confusion, squires and servants running in all directions through the half-light of early morning. Armed soldiers were moving more purposefully towards the edge of the camp that faced the enemy. The clear call of the trumpet sounded over the noise, issuing instructions to the men which Zaphreth could not interpret. The worst sounds of all came from the direction of the horn and the edge of the camp: the clash of weaponry, hoarse shouting, and screams of pain.

Zaphreth's pounding heart wanted him to run, to head away from the fighting and find a quiet hole where he could cower until it was all over. But he did not know the camp, and an annoying part of his mind wondered where Runa was and whether she was safe. He should not care about the northerners, he knew. But he did.

"Zaphreth!" Runa waved at him, darting out of King Mabrigas's tent, narrowly avoiding collision with a squire carrying an armful of spears, and ducking around another bearing a shield and short sword.

"Oi!" the shield-bearer shouted at her. "What are you kids doing here? We're under attack – go to the back of the camp and get out of here!"

"What made them attack?" Runa gasped, grabbing at Zaphreth's arm. He was preparing to run into the camp, as the squire had ordered, but she dragged him back, pulling him behind a tent. "It violates every code of war!"

Guilt sat sick and cold in the pit of his stomach, and Zaphreth fought the urge to vomit. He had brought about the attack, by Sending to Lord Lur in the night.

Horses' hooves crushed the grass around them as the tSardian cavalry overran the camp, followed swiftly by the foot-soldiers.

Crouching behind a tent with Runa, Zaphreth fought the desire to clamp his hands about his ears. He could hear the dull squelch of weapons driving into flesh, and the frightened gasps of squires as they fought against experienced soldiers and riders.

Like a drift of old leaves, memories of his training scattered through his mind. Zaphreth blushed at his boastful ambition, his ideas of driving through enemy lines and driving back the Callenlasians. He knew, just listening to the conflict on the other side of the tent, that he was no soldier. He was not sure now that he ever could drive a blade through another person.

After a while, the battle moved away from where they hid, and Runa led Zaphreth out. Her face was pale, her eyes huge, but there was a grim set to her mouth.

"This way," she said.

"Where are you going?" Zaphreth hissed, for she was heading towards the tSardian camp.

"I want to see what's happening," Runa said. "We're not in danger here now."

"That could change," Zaphreth said grimly, even while his admiration for Runa swelled. She was fearless, leading the way through the tents and up a small rise at the edge of the camp, where they could oversee what was happening.

"Just ... hang on a second!" Zaphreth grabbed at her

wrist and pulled Runa up short.

"Quickly!" she urged. "Before my father's servers drag me away!"

"Isn't this what got you into trouble in the first place?" Zaphreth asked.

Runa turned to glare at him, her lips compressed in stubborn irritation. Suddenly she relented, like a sail falling slack after a gust of wind. She crossed her arms and poked the dust with her toe.

"I wish you weren't right," she grumbled. "Don't you want to see what's happening?"

No! thought Zaphreth, but he could hardly admit that to a girl.

"We should go to safety," he said.

Without warning, a vast shadow rippled over the tents around them, cast by a great black flying over from the tSardian side. A jet of flame spurted down, incinerating the tents to Zaphreth's left, and causing a fire which quickly spread behind them.

"Now we are running for safety!" Runa grinned, as they headed in the direction she had wanted to go in the first place.

Zaphreth shook his head but had little choice, with the heat of the flames pursuing them, and the gust of the dragon's wings stirring the dust all around them.

At the edge of the camp, they crouched between

the last line of tents, finding a handful that remained undamaged from the attack. After a gap of about thirty paces, a slope ran upwards away from them, grown over with some prickly gorse, protected from tramping feet by a collection of stubby, twisted trees that were barely taller than Zaphreth.

Zaphreth peered out, checking for soldiers. This was just the kind of place where cowardly men might hide out until the battle was over. He could see nothing, however, and together, in a crouch, he and Runa ran for the slope. They ducked under the shadow of the gorse.

Behind them to their left, the battle raged within the camp, tents half-fallen and standing at peculiar angles, bloodstained or trampled. Skirmishes were occurring in the gaps between tents, the two armies meeting each other unexpectedly around corners, clashing in the ashes of campfires or in the wider spaces reserved for drills.

But while they had been running from the dragon, King Elior had mounted his white charger and driven through the tSardian ranks. At the back of the battle, to the south, he searched until he found Lord Lur.

They met in the desert plain just below Runa and Zaphreth, and were now engaged in single combat.

Watching breathlessly over the spiky gorse bush, Runa and Zaphreth saw Lur facing Elior with a gap of twenty paces between them. For a moment, Zaphreth's belief in the humanity of the two figures persisted. They seemed so small, Elior's head slightly bowed as though reluctant to fight. Then Lur flicked his left hand as though brushing off a fly and a wave of force travelled through the air. It would have floored any human within thirty paces, but King Elior simply raised his hand and deflected it.

The tiny actions made Zaphreth feel dizzy, his entire world shifting as he realised the truth of everything Runa had said. The two figures were stars, wielding immense power. Zaphreth swallowed.

"You chose to come as a man," Elior called, drawing his sword. "Fight like one."

In answer, Lur twisted his other hand and produced an emerald fireball. He hurled it at the King, who extinguished it and ran towards Lur, sword upheld.

"You cannot win," Elior warned, but winning or losing were long forgotten in Lur's thoughts. He aimed a sheet of violet fire at the running King, and a hail of icy arrows, but then the King was upon him, and their swords clashed.

Some among both armies had noticed the fight between their two leaders. They had ceased their own battle to range around the warring stars, at a distance. A cheer rose from Elior's men, who had been silent until now.

The two figures wrestled; swords pressed together over their heads, the dust rising in clouds around their scuffling feet. Then they broke apart and exchanged a few testing blows with their blades before Lur threw another wave of force at Elior. The King allowed it to pass over him, then drove his sword into Lur's side, just under the ribs.

Runa cheered, pumping the air with her fist; Zaphreth choked on his own breath, but the warlord did not fall.

He lifted his sword and attacked again, to cheers from the tSardian army.

"That blow should have killed him," Zaphreth gaped.

"You can't kill a star," Runa said, as if it was something he should have known.

"What happens to them then?"

"They heal quicker than us," Runa replied. "But if their injuries are too many, they must be unbodied, or live in constant pain."

"Why doesn't Elior just 'unbody' Lur now, and win?"

"It is an act of great violence, unless the star consents," Runa replied. "How do you not know all this?"

"We were taught it was a myth. Why would we learn the details of a made-up story?"

"Made-up?!"

But discussions about philosophy had to be delayed. Lur was driving King Elior back now, seemingly oblivious to the blood pouring down his left leg. He had sustained another injury also, to his right shoulder, but had simply switched his sword to his left hand and fought on without missing a beat. Elior also appeared to be injured, but only lightly, a scrape to his right thigh.

Lur now raised his injured hand and a glow of emerald light shimmered in the air, fingers ebbing forward, reaching for the King.

Elior sent out a bolt of blue light which met the emerald, but instead of shattering it the two forces met and entwined like wrestlers, strength against strength.

The swords lay forgotten in the dust as the two stars blazed in the centre of the plain, all but extinguished by the display of their own power. The light grew too bright, and Runa and Zaphreth were forced to first shield their eyes and then look away. Zaphreth trembled at the power.

There was a sound like a distant explosion, and then a rush of warm air passed over the hill, shifting Zaphreth's hair, making his ears pulse as if he had been ducked underwater.

He sat up the instant it had passed to find the plain as it had been before, lit only by the Day-Star. Where the two stars had stood, a circle of charred earth surrounded them, ten paces across. Lur's body lay on the floor at the feet of King Elior.

A cheer rose from the northern army, and Runa joined them, jumping up and down and waving her arms ecstatically. Zaphreth sat dumbfounded, staring at his fallen leader, but also at the figure of the King he had always hated. Elior stood over his enemy, not elated but still, his head bowed. Zaphreth, still awed by the sheer power exhibited by the two figures, felt fingers of fear creeping around his heart. If King Elior could destroy Lord Lur, what would he do to a boy found guilty of betrayal?

The tSardian army was beginning to flee south, back to their camp. When the Callenlasians began to make chase, King Elior called them back. He sent men back to the camp, to declare victory to those still fighting there.

"Is he dead?" Zaphreth asked, leaning over the tussock to look more closely at his fallen Lord. He could not keep the fear from his voice, even though he knew it might betray him.

"I told you – stars can't die!" Runa laughed, elated in victory. "He's probably unconscious."

"Will he be ... unbodied ... now?"

"I expect he will be taken prisoner and sentenced properly," Runa said.

Zaphreth drew deep breaths. Perhaps he should slip south now, run back to Ama. But what would happen to Irek? Perhaps if he kept up his pretence a little longer, he could plead for his father, and then they could both escape to the south once the peace treaty was settled.

Runa had grabbed Zaphreth's hand and was dragging him back towards the camp. He followed limply, his mind in turmoil.

CHAPTER 23

Sitting astride a small horse, Runa ambled along the road north to Orr, a song in her heart. The banners of King Elior fluttered all along the column of soldiers, interspersed with the flags of various noble houses. She was riding among a cluster of amber and gold flags, with the Feldemoorian cohort. Father rode further back with his generals and advisors, but Runa had escaped that company as early as she could. She was hoping to find Zaphreth, but the boy had been surprisingly quiet and evasive since King Elior's victory.

Runa had badgered her father for an hour to be allowed to travel to Orr with the few of his party who would join King Elior in settling the peace terms with tSardia and passing judgement on Lord Lur. King Mabrigas had been all for sending her north by dragon and shutting her up safely in one of the palaces.

"I'm not a child!" Runa had protested. "I survived shipwreck, a forest, and capture! I deserve to come!"

Something in King Mabrigas's face had changed. It was almost as if, Runa thought, he *saw* her for the first time. As if he had always seen her as a princess, but never as Runa.

"Then you should come," he said simply. He spoiled the moment by adding, "but you *must* behave yourself!"

This was now the third day of the seven-day journey to Orr, and they had left the desert behind at last. Here great fields of wheat and barley spread all around them, the plains of Callenlas that had swept beneath Runa while she slept on her dragon journey from the forests. She wished now that she could join the dragons which patrolled overhead, with their clear view of the plains which rolled from Meretharnae, the forest, all the way to the western Waste, and the fabled city of Iliathtil.

Somewhere to the front of the long column of soldiers was King Elior, riding tall, and near him, bound with chains and the force of three Masters' minds, Lord Lur was carried in a covered cage.

Runa shuddered to think how he had deceived so many, taking the form of a man, copying the other stars who had come to earth. She wondered how people had been so easily taken in. S*he* would have known he was not to be trusted ... wouldn't she?

The memory of Uncle Izzecha drifted uncomfortably into her mind, and Runa was confronted with the realisation that good and evil were not always so easily distinguishable as in books and stories.

Uncle Izzecha was also bound, though not so securely as the dark star. Shortly the road would fork, and he would be carried north to Feldemoore, to be imprisoned on the remote island of Bracha. It was a three-day sea voyage from the northern coast of Feldemoore, and while pretty, it was very small, and often cut off from the world by strong winds and storms. Runa felt the comforting weight of satisfaction on her chest. Uncle Izzecha's betrayal still hurt her, the worse for his kindness. She felt glad and sorry that he would be so far away.

It was late afternoon, and from the front of the column came the orders to make camp for the evening, but not in the fields of wheat, for that would destroy the farmers' crop. Ahead lay a stretch of pastureland. Tonight, they would sleep among sheep and cows.

Runa was at last beginning to feel that sense of adventure she had always imagined. Riding across open plains, listening to the songs of soldiers, eating around campfires, sleeping under the stars. This was what she was made for.

80 ∗ CR

Watching the early light throw long shadows over the tent walls, Zaphreth's mind sleepily drifted back to Ama. He wondered what she was doing, whether she was still going through the morning routine that had woken him after so many dawns; raking the charcoal to flame in the hearth, setting the pan to heat, lifting the plates and cups down from their shelf, ready for breakfast.

But perhaps she had left the little hut now. Perhaps the hearth stood empty, the remains of her last, lonely fire crumbling to ash. Perhaps she had gathered up her meagre belongings and walked into Sarreia to beg. Perhaps ... perhaps she simply was not anywhere any more.

That thought was too terrible to complete and Zaphreth scrunched his eyes closed, wishing he had not allowed himself to think of Ama.

What now drifted into his unwilling mind was the memory of their argument. He had pushed this memory down carefully, piling the busyness of his training and the urgency of his mission for Lord Lur heavily on top of it. Even now he did not want to remember, but the stillness of the morning made it impossible to keep the memory quiet any longer. His inner misery seemed to erupt as he lay on his pallet, listening to the quiet stirring of the camp.

He had come home from the city that day with his

head held high, a Servant of Lur, ready to train to serve him. Zaphreth had stood in the doorway of the hut, dressed in the black novice's robes given to him before he left the General's quarters, the creases sharp, the fabric stiff with newness.

"What have you done?" Ama's face lost its colour, and she folded like a ragdoll onto the stool by the fire.

"The king's General wants me in his service," Zaphreth said, trying to speak like a man. Annoyingly, his voice squeaked most when he tried hardest to speak evenly.

Ama stared at him, aghast.

"But you are just a boy," she whispered.

"I am a man," Zaphreth asserted. "As of today. And I could not bear to sit here, doing nothing, while men like father fight for our country."

"For our country?" a rare flash of anger blazed up in her eyes. "We had everything we needed before this war started! What lies have you been fed?"

"Lies?" Zaphreth scoffed. "You can tell me about lies, can't you? Who was my mother?"

"What?" Ama stared at him, bewildered.

"Tell me, who was my mother?" Zaphreth demanded, with jutted out chin and clenched fists. He glared at her, all the thoughts that had tumbled through his mind on the long walk back from Sarreia catching suddenly like deadwood.

"Who told you ...?"

"That doesn't matter. Why didn't you tell me the truth?"

"The truth ..."

"My mother was your sister, wasn't she?"

There was an appalled silence, then, "Yes," Ama whispered, tears spilling over. She clutched at her apron, bunching it and releasing it in her left fist. Her eyes flicked back and forth like a trapped animal and Zaphreth had a vague sense that he was being cruel, but he was too angry to restrain himself.

"Why didn't you tell me?"

"She died, Zaphreth. Rusi died when you were born. She never even held you ... I was your mother from your first breath," Ama rocked on her stool, unable to contain the grief she had held in for fourteen years. "We couldn't have children. You were a gift from the stars, from Rusi."

"Why didn't you tell me?" Zaphreth raged, slamming his hand into the table. "Why didn't you tell me about my father?"

"To what purpose?" Ama wailed. "You were ours, truly ours! Your father did not deserve that name – he cared nothing for you – he abandoned Rusi as soon as he knew about you! She was helpless, so we took her in, despite the shame. And then she died, my sweet Rusi ..."

Zaphreth's blood still thundered in his ears and his

chest heaved.

"You should have told me," he said.

"I'm sorry," Ama sobbed, but now she knelt on the floor, crabbing towards his feet, clutching at the fringe of his new tunic. Her fingers were grubby from sweeping the floors of the rich, and Zaphreth took an instinctive step back. He wanted his uniform pristine for the morning.

"Oh Zaphreth," she pleaded, "Don't go. Don't leave me ... I'll have nothing!"

"We have nothing now!" he raged. He gripped her by the arms and hoisted her up, shaking her like a child. "Can't you see? We have nothing now! At least I am doing something, fighting! We have money, look—" Zaphreth released her, and drew out his first pay from his purse. He slapped the silver onto the table with a sharp crack.

Ama stared at it.

"I don't want it," she spat bitterly. "Blood money!"

And now she saw the bandage around Zaphreth's hand.

"What happened?" she demanded, gripping his fingers.

"Nothing," he said, looking away from her.

"You swore in blood?" she whispered, staring at him. "Oh, Zaphreth."

"I told you, the king's General wants me for his service. Don't you see what an honour that is?"

254

"But to swear in blood ... you know your life is his now?"

"Better than belonging to this family."

The words hung bitter in the air, and Ama looked as though she had been slapped. Zaphreth almost wished he *had* slapped her instead, but his anger made the words feel true, and he did not know how to take them back.

"I'm going to bed," he said at last, careening up the ladder to his small attic – his *shelf*, he corrected himself sourly – where the weathered, wooden tiles gaped to give him narrow sight of the stars. He could hear Ama shuffling about, and finally the scuff of her sleeping mat being unrolled, and then the puff of the lamp as she blew it out.

In the tent, beneath the Callenlasian banner, Zaphreth groaned and curled himself into a tight ball. How many weeks had passed since that argument, since the next morning when he coldly kissed Ama's cheek before walking out of the little house. He had little doubt that she had watched him all along the road to Sarreia. He had deliberately not looked back.

He had thought he was being brave, powerful, dynamic, pushing aside the fretful worries of a fearful woman, crushed by poverty.

Now, in the morning light, Zaphreth wondered if the most courageous thing might have been to stay at home.

The thought was like letting a cat slowly unfurl her claws inside his heart. It made him want to pull the blankets over his head with shame. He had been heartless, he realised, with an awful shudder. He had thought only of himself, while pretending to be so noble and brave. All he had wanted really was to escape the poverty of the hut, and his parents.

It certainly would have been better for those who had died in the final attack. Facing the truth of this was like being slugged in the chest, and for a moment Zaphreth could not breathe. The evening after the battle an eerie hush had blanketed the camp. Fallen tents had been picked up, horses calmed, wounds bandaged. The bodies of the fallen had been laid in long lines. As the Day-Star's light faded, the tSardians came and collected their own.

Then King Elior had stepped up and raised his hands over the fallen Callenlasians, lying in sombre rows on the dusty soil.

"Blessed are you," he had spoken, with tears glittering on his cheeks and in his beard. "You who have given everything for your people. May your souls be welcomed into the Fields of Light. And may your bodies be dispersed to dust, until the end of all things."

As the light of the Day-Star disappeared beneath the horizon, and the first stars began to fleck the sky like scattered diamonds, the air over the bodies began to stir as the souls rose swirling into the night, like glittering smoke. The bodies followed, disintegrating to dust, rising on the air to dance like smoke against the sky.

Zaphreth had been overtaken by the beauty and solemnity of the moment, until he had remembered, with a nauseating jolt, all the families left behind by the dead. The scale of it overwhelmed him as he watched all the hundreds of souls rising, drifting, their bodies lost. Perhaps it was a comfort to think of them welcomed to feast with the stars in the Fields of Light. But still, there were homes left without fathers, brothers, husbands, sons ... and all because of him.

Zaphreth groaned again, knowing himself now to be the most miserable person beneath the stars. Because if what Runa said was true, then the stars watched human behaviour. They had seen. They could whisper to King Elior all that he had done. They would know that he had Sent to Lord Lur.

What could he do? Zaphreth swallowed hard and chewed on his lower lip. The only thing he could do, he realised, was get through the next few weeks without drawing the King's attention, then sneak back to tSardia when it was all over. It seemed that King Elior was willing to let people go. He could keep up the lie of wanting to be a Callenlasian for a few more days, then Runa would go home and he could just slip away. He might even find

Irek among the prisoners of war, and they could go back to Ama.

Although, of course, his father would be listed as a vine tender which would reveal his lie. Zaphreth pressed his curled hands against his temples. What a mess he was in! No, he must just keep out of sight and make his way back to Sarreia as soon as he could. He would find Irek and Ama there, and they could make a new life.

He could take his claim to the king, the humbled Lakesh, retreating hastily to his palaces and pleasures in tSama. Yes, that was it. He would get away from here as soon as he could, find his parents, appeal to King Lakesh for his rights as Prince Zaphreth, and then live in a palace in peace, and forget all about Callenlas, Runa, and King Elior.

He tried very hard to ignore the rather sharp pain that pressed the centre of his chest, and the sense of emptiness that filled him at the thought of such a future. There was no other choice, he told himself firmly. If he told King Elior the truth, he would be executed as a traitor. Even King Elior could not be kind to someone who had brought about so much death and pain.

CHAPTER 24

Orr had been built in the east of the plains of Callenlas, surrounded by rich farmland, with the trees of Meretharnae within sight. Its walls were built of a curious pale stone which appeared a dull, sand colour close up, but from a distance caught the light of the Day-Star so that it glimmered like pale gold. The walls were the height of six men, sheer and smooth so they could not be climbed, and behind them the city rose in tiers, like a mountain built of houses and palaces.

The company rode beneath the great gates to find cheering crowds flinging petals into the air and waving brightly coloured ribbons. The houses were decked with the banners of King Elior and Callenlas, white emblazoned with a star of gold. Children ran and skipped along with the procession, scooping up handfuls of fallen petals to throw them in the air again.

Runa beamed and waved, thoroughly enjoying herself. Zaphreth waved too, but inside his misery only grew. The cheers were not for him. If they knew what he had done, they would roar and hiss as they did when Lur was carried through.

The following day Lur's judgement was pronounced. A large wooden platform had been erected just outside the city, so that any could see it who wished to. There was also a great crowd of tSardian prisoners, those who had been kept at the city while the war progressed. They stood together, surrounded by King Elior's guards, but none seemed particularly fearful. A few wore an expression of resentment, or boredom, but there was almost a holiday atmosphere among all gathered; prisoners, soldiers and citizens alike.

Zaphreth scouted for his father, but the sea of faces were too many for him to distinguish individuals. He had found himself on the platform with all the official attendants, next to Runa, dressed in a squire's uniform in the colours of Elior, white with a dark blue and gold trim. He had thought it best to say as little as possible, and was just drifting, carried along by everyone around him, particularly Runa. She was wearing the colours of Feldemoore; a burnt orange dress with a cloak of gold. She looked regal, despite the slight snub of her nose under its smattering of freckles. Zaphreth wondered how he had not seen her dignity before, and how no one had noticed his lack of it yet.

Lur was carried onto the platform, his arrival heralding hisses and shouts of 'long live King Elior' from the crowd. He was sitting in a chair of wrought metal, his wrists and ankles bound with glowing violet bonds. The crowd fell silent, but Zaphreth could feel the hatred directed at the warlord from the people.

King Elior stepped forward and smiled gravely at his people.

"Friends," he proclaimed. "We have come to establish justice and peace once more upon this island. Much has been lost, and we will mourn the lives that have been sacrificed on both sides of the border for many years.

"But I trust that our brothers in the south have seen that the true instigator of war has been this Lur, the darkened star. By cunning and evil he persuaded you that war was just, and my rule unfair and wrong. I trust you can see otherwise now.

"First, I speak to those of my own people who have fought bravely and given all for their countrymen. Your courage and love are celebrated today and will be remembered."

Here a great cheer rose from the people gathered before the platform. Flags waved and more confetti was thrown, and the applause continued for a long while. King Elior clapped with them, smiling at his people warmly. At last, he raised his hands and silence rippled back over the crowd.

"Now I address those who have fought against us and been captured. You know how you have been treated, with kindness and generosity. I now give you your freedom. You may remain, if you wish to pledge your loyalty to me, and live as free citizens of Callenlas. If you have a wife and children, you may send for them. If you wish to return to your home in tSardia then I grant you your freedom also, but I ask one thing. Remember the kindness and generosity you have received while in my custody. Remember who has granted you your freedom. Remember who has shown you mercy. And do not lift your hand against me again.

"When the judgment is over, move forward to speak to my scribes who will make note of your decision."

Zaphreth could not take his eyes off the King. This was the first time he had been so physically close to him, and Zaphreth was struggling to fit the wisdom and kindness of his words to the image he had grown up with. In a moment both terrible and wonderful, he faced the realisation that King Elior was everything he had thought Lur would be and had failed to find in him. The realisation was like an ember burning in the centre of his chest. He had found what he had been looking for, someone worth following ... and now he would have to leave it behind, sneak off to the south and the desert.

"Now," King Elior turned to Lur, and an ugly snarl crossed the dark star's face. "Lur, I charge you with treachery against myself, the King of Callenlas, and the chosen Lord over these people, and your rightful Lord by all the universal laws of the Council of Stars. I charge you with treachery against the people you called your own, and the King of tSardia. I charge you with using forces of magic against my rightful rule. You are a liar, a deceiver and a thief. You have caused misery and death to thousands in tSardia and Callenlas and sought to draw in many more nations to the mess of war you created. I grant you no mercy, no right of appeal. You are hereby banished from this land and are cursed to wander the Fields of Light with no resting place, until the conclusion of all things is known. You will be unbodied here, today.

"Do you have any final words?"

Lur's expression was one of pure hatred and disdain. He surveyed the crowds, his eyes glowing red, that inner flame no longer concealed.

"You are fools," he spat. "I offer you freedom, liberty! And you run, like frightened children, back to this pathetic King who will insist on obedience to his miserable laws."

"You offer no freedom," King Elior countered, his voice calm but strong. "Only the oppression of anarchy. Prepare yourself, Lur."

"Wait," Lur spoke, quieter. His eyes now turned to the

crowd of nobles and scribes gathered on the platform. To Zaphreth's horror, Lur's gaze fell on him, and a cruel grin spread across his face. "That one is mine," Lur said. "He is bound to me by his own blood. If I go, he goes with me, and all others who made such an oath."

Zaphreth's heart was pounding, and there was a strange roaring in his ears. His fingers tingled, and for a moment he thought he would faint. But there was no such relief. All about him were staring at him; even King Elior had turned to look.

"Come forward," he summoned.

Fists clenched, Zaphreth did the bravest thing he had ever done. He thought his legs would give way, but he stepped away from the crowd gathered at the back of the platform and stood before the King. As he did, he caught a glimpse of Runa's face, white, with a glint of horror in her green eyes.

"Is this true?" King Elior asked. Zaphreth squinted up at him suddenly, for the King's voice was heavy with sorrow, when Zaphreth had expected anger. In answer, Zaphreth extended his left palm and revealed the scar.

King Elior closed his eyes.

"Will you never be satisfied?" he asked of Lur. "Will your lust for blood and pain never be quenched?"

Lur said nothing, but sat back with a smirk.

The King lowered his head and stood silent for a long

time. Zaphreth wondered what his judgement would be. In his view there was no question; Lur must be unbodied and removed from the earth. And so he, Zaphreth, must die with him. He knew he deserved it too. He had been as much a deceiver as Lur. He hung his head and waited for the King to pronounce the death sentence.

Then a shout came from the crowd, small with distance. Someone was fighting their way through the prisoners, arms flailing like a poor swimmer as he made his way through the closely packed men.

"My son!" the cry reached them at last. "That's my son."

Zaphreth's shame reached a peak. He crumpled to the boards, warmed by the Day-Star, and wept.

He did not see the guards trying to prevent Irek from scrambling up onto the platform, nor King Elior gesturing for them to step back. His father stumbled to him, scooping him up like a little boy. Zaphreth's face was pressed against his brown beard and the soft roughness of the woollen tunic he wore. He smelled different, of grain and woodsmoke, but the voice was the same.

"This is my son," Irek cried to King Elior. "I give my life for him."

"No!" Zaphreth fought his father's embrace. "No!"

"Enough," King Elior said, neither roughly nor sharply, but with an authority that brought them both to silence.

"Enough lives have been lost."

The King turned gravely to face Lur once more.

"I give you one undefended blow against me, for all the lives bound to you. You may make one strike against me. Immediately after you will be unbodied and banished to the darkness between the stars. Do you accept?"

Lur's expression was one of triumph.

"I accept."

"No," Zaphreth whispered desperately to his father, still blinded by the tears in his eyes. "No – he cannot! He doesn't know what I did ..."

But Zaphreth's father was drawing him back, away from the centre of the platform. The ropes about Lur's hands and feet were released and Elior was holding out his sword, grip first, to him.

Zaphreth felt as though his heart would burst, but he was frozen to the spot as Lur, with a cry of conquest, thrust the sword right through the heart of King Elior. Blood poured red onto the bleached boards and the King staggered.

Lur extracted the sword and raised it above his head, the blood dripping onto his face and streaming down his forearms. Violet light began to shine from him, pulsing and growing brighter until he was unbearable to look upon. His form began to change, his skin blackening and contorting as though it had been only a wax covering, now melting.

For a heartbeat there was the dark outline of a man in the centre of a blaze of light, and then, with a blinding flash and a shriek of rage and pain, he was gone.

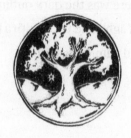

CHAPTER 25

Zaphreth stared numbly at the fallen figure of the King, trying not to notice his blood pooling thickly on the sanded boards. His father's arms held him tightly as those gathered on the platform rushed forward. A bier was brought, and in eerie silence Elior was carried inside the city.

For a moment Zaphreth had a wild hope of slipping away with his father – certainly Irek was tugging him towards the steps, off the platform, towards the crowd. But then Mabrigas caught Zaphreth's eye and smiled invitingly, and servants and squires were bowing and making a way for Zaphreth through the press, to follow the royal family behind the bier.

Finding he had no choice, Zaphreth walked in the silent procession, his thoughts a whirlwind. Irek walked with him, the solemnity of the crowd forbidding any questions for the moment.

The King's stretcher was carried into the palace, and away. Zaphreth and Irek were pulled along by the Feldemoorian party, up staircases, towards King Mabrigas's rooms.

Zaphreth fought to think sensibly. So far, everyone knew he was Prince Herodas's heir, Lord of Talivera. Everyone except Irek. Zaphreth cringed inside at the thought of telling Irek, whose arms were now still supporting him tightly, that he knew he was not his real father. But it would have to be done. Surely once Irek realised that Zaphreth could now provide the lovely home Ama had always wanted, he would be glad. He would be no less Zaphreth's father.

But of course, Runa had told everyone that Zaphreth had run away from tSardia to sign up with King Elior, so that pretence must be maintained, somehow, as well.

Perhaps, Zaphreth thought, he could say he wanted to return to tSardia, now the war was over, to help build friendship between the two countries. He wanted that anyway, he realised, with a faint lightening of the shadow on his heart. As long as no one found out that he had Sent information to Lur ...

Reaching the king's rooms, Irek hesitated, expecting to be directed elsewhere, but King Mabrigas again gave them a look of invitation.

"I ... I think I'd like to go to my rooms, my King," Zaphreth managed to say, with something like confidence.

"Of course," Mabrigas began with his usual courtesy, but Runa leaped forward, green eyes ablaze.

"Oh no you don't!" she exclaimed; every inch of her frame filled with fury. "You *lied* to me! You lied to everyone! You were working for Lord Lur the whole time!"

Zaphreth stammered, his cheeks flushing darkly, and King Mabrigas held Runa back.

"Runa," he rebuked gently.

"No, father," she raged. "He's a liar and a sneak – a traitor!"

"Runa!" Mabrigas's voice was stern. "I will not have you throw about insults and hard words without knowing the full facts."

He turned his gaze upon Zaphreth.

"Go and rest," he said. "I will talk to Runa, and we will speak again later."

"Yes, my King," Zaphreth nodded. As he turned, something whistled past his head, smashing into the wall just behind him, a missile hurled by the outraged Runa.

"I'm afraid I will have to set a guard at your door, for now," King Mabrigas called, trying to push the flailing Runa back into his room.

"Of course," Zaphreth bowed, feeling as though his

270

mind and body had been set at a distance.

"Zaphreth," King Mabrigas called, as an afterthought. "Zaphreth, the King is not dead."

"He's not?"

"He is a star. His life is different to ours."

"Runa told me," Zaphreth poked the toe of his shoe into the pile of the carpet at his feet, remembering her scorn at his ignorance. *Stars can't die.*

"His injury is great. Lur did as much damage as he could, and for a normal man it would be a mortal blow. In fact, for most stars it would mean their human life must end, and they must return to the Fields of Light. But King Elior is no ordinary star. He will repair, but it will take time."

Whatever had been compressing Zaphreth's ribcage was released a little, and he drew an easier breath.

"What will he do to me?" he asked, hardly daring to speak.

"What Runa does not understand, and what will be explained to her as soon as she calms down enough to listen, is the immense pressure you were under to obey Lur. I am not saying you had no fault in it at all, but Lur can hold great sway over the hearts of men. He used magic to turn men's minds and hearts to his purpose, and while those arts may be resisted, it takes great strength.

"The King knows your heart, Zaphreth. Fear not.

271

When he is recovered, he will make a decision that is both just and merciful. Until then, rest. Tell your father all that has happened to you."

Zaphreth nodded, and the king drew back into his room. Suddenly weary, Zaphreth turned back to his father and the servant.

"Would you show us to my rooms, please," Zaphreth asked, with all the dignity he could muster.

"Of course, my Lord," the servant bowed and led Zaphreth and his father through a series of rooms. At last, a door appeared that Zaphreth recognised, and he thanked the servant.

"Shall I fetch food, my Lord? Hot water for a bath?"

"Not now, thank you."

Zaphreth and his father entered the room, and then closed the door.

For a moment they stared at each other, as strangers.

"What have you got yourself into then, lad?" Irek asked at last, easing himself into one of the chairs near the empty fireplace, and fixing a sympathetic but probing look upon his son.

Zaphreth sank into the chair opposite and covered his face with his hands.

"Why are you suddenly friends with royals? And how did you come to be sold to the General?"

"I gave myself to the General on oath," Zaphreth

answered. He held out his left hand to show the scar across his palm.

Irek's face showed concern.

"What led you to do that, son?" he asked. "What could a fourteen-year-old do in battle?"

"I thought ... I thought I could help end the war. And then the General told me ..." Zaphreth could hardly bear to say it, with Irek sitting right before him. "He told me about my real father."

"Your real ..." Irek's voice dried up and he leaned back in his seat, drawing in a sharp breath. "I see."

"Lord Lur told me I could inherit my father's lands; become Lord of Talivera."

"Lord of Talivera?" confusion creased Irek's features.

"Yes; he said if I served him well now, then he would speak to King Lakesh and have my lands restored to me. I hope the king might still honour the request, for I did my best to serve tSardia. That's why I came here, see. Lord Lur wanted information – "

"Slow down," Irek held up his hands. "One thing at a time. Who do you think your father was?"

"Prince Herodas, brother to King Lakesh," Zaphreth said with an air of impatience. "You were there! You should know!"

"I do know," Irek said, slowly. "It seems Lord Lur was lying to you."

Zaphreth felt the room spin, and he gripped the arms of his chair.

"He said my mother, Ama's sister, served in Prince Herodas' household."

"She was a floor-sweeper in the household of Sir Lobras, a scribe for the prince's chancellor. I am certain that she never met the prince – she would never have been allowed into his presence."

Zaphreth had to swallow several times before he could speak. He wanted so badly to be important. He *needed* to be important. He could not go back to the watchman's hut, to the workshop, and scuttling out of the way like a cockroach whenever anyone of significance walked by.

"So, my father is ...?"

"We believe it was Sir Lobras, though Rusi would never speak of it. He would have nothing to do with her, though she pleaded with him for help. In fact, it was he who commanded that she be thrown out of his household."

"I'm not a prince," Zaphreth's voice was barely a whisper.

"No," Irek said.

All Zaphreth's dreams and plans swayed before him, like a great tower, before crumbling into the dust. A desperate part of his mind scrambled for threads of hope, for the possibility that Rusi had, after all, met

Prince Lakesh. But he knew it was hopeless. No floor-sweeper was permitted in the presence of the prince, however beautiful.

He was a nobody after all. The illegitimate, unwanted son of a scribe. A poor apprentice. A failed soldier.

Zaphreth swallowed hard. He closed his eyes against the realisation that he had been lording it over Runa, an actual princess, on false information. He had thought himself so important.

And now ... now nothing was left except to slink back to the south, to the dreary hut on the edge of the cursed desert, disgraced, rejected – and a painful lump came into his throat at this thought – rejected by the only people who had ever shown him real kindness.

But there was worse.

"I've been thinking, actually," Irek said, tentatively, his eyes on Zaphreth, watching for his reaction. "I wonder about taking up King Elior's offer to us prisoners of war. Especially as you're here. It would be easy to fetch Ama up here. Don't you think she'd like it? A little house somewhere, with a garden. A few goats. There might even be a vineyard that needs tending somewhere abouts."

Zaphreth wanted to howl. Not only had he thrown away his own hopes of ever prospering, but he had now destroyed his parents'. King Elior would never allow a traitor, a spy, a rebel, to remain in Callenlas. He might even unbody him if he found out about Zaphreth's betrayal.

"I don't think King Elior would want me," is what mumbled out of his mouth, while his gaze remained fixed on the floor at his feet. "After what I did. Lying and all."

"Well, he's forgiven all the other prisoners of war, everyone else Lur deceived. I don't see why not you too?"

"No, father," Zaphreth shook his head in misery. "This cannot be made better. You don't know what I have done!"

"And I think you have not understood the King. Remember what he did for you, Zaphreth. He took that sword for you."

"Not just for me," Zaphreth sniffed.

"But yes, for you. You were the one kneeling before him, sentenced to death."

Zaphreth shook his head.

"He didn't know what I had done then."

"What have you done?" Irek cried. "Tell me, I am your father."

Zaphreth shook his head. It was too awful. He kept thinking of the line of dead on the plain, husbands, fathers, sons ... all the men who had died because he had told Lur to attack. He kept thinking of Elior's face, the sorrow in his words, *how many more lives must be lost? How much more blood must be shed?*

Yet King Mabrigas, and his father, had been so certain of King Elior's mercy. Perhaps he could plead, perhaps he would only be imprisoned, or even sent back to tSardia. He could start over; become an apprentice again.

The thought was appalling, too miserable for words, but better, Zaphreth supposed, than being unbodied.

For a while, he allowed himself to feel sorry for the big house and servants and gold that he felt he had lost. Then slowly, the memory of mornings in the hut with Ama and Irek seeped into his mind. It had not been all bad. The days when there was not enough food had been dreadful, but there had been cheerful mornings when the Day-Star streamed through the little window, and Ama sang as she raked the charcoal and laid the breadpan over the heat, when Irek had found a spare copper to give to Zaphreth to buy sweets in the market.

Perhaps, Zaphreth thought, perhaps it was possible to be happy, even without very much.

৪০ ✳ ୧୫

The days that followed were horrible for Zaphreth. His imagination cast all sorts of shadows onto the walls of his room, from a vision of himself blasted apart by an angry King Elior, to him managing to hide his awful secret and living on a Callenlasian farm with his parents. That one

277

was hardest to maintain.

Guilt crouched darkly inside his gut, especially when King Mabrigas came to see him, determined to believe the best about Zaphreth. He kept saying how Lord Lur was powerful, and able to persuade the best of men, but all Zaphreth kept thinking was how glad he had been to follow the evil General, in the hope of getting something for himself.

"The King is doing better than expected," King Mabrigas said, and Zaphreth was surprised by the warmth that spread through his anxious chest.

"I'm glad to hear it," Zaphreth said. It was a relief to speak words he meant whole-heartedly.

"Now, I'm sorry I have to ask this, Zaphreth," Mabrigas sighed, leaning forwards. "Did you intend harm against the King?"

"No," Zaphreth replied earnestly. "I only had to find out things. Information."

King Mabrigas nodded slowly.

"I'm afraid the guard will have to remain over your door for now, but once the King is well enough, he will see you, and everything will be worked out."

The kindness made it worse, Zaphreth decided. If they had all decided to hate him for his deception, then he could just hate them back.

"You have no need to fear," King Mabrigas went on.

"King Elior will do what is just."

Zaphreth's experience of justice was public whippings and long prison sentences, even slavery or death. He chewed on his lip, wondering what form the justice of King Elior would take.

"Is Runa ...?" Zaphreth hardly knew how to phrase his question.

"Runa is still very angry," King Mabrigas said, with a regretful smile, "And hurt. My daughter is hot-headed, and stubborn, but she is also kind. She will calm down, eventually, I am sure."

Zaphreth had his doubts. He had seen the flame in Runa's eyes as she was pulled back within the Feldemoorian chambers.

King Mabrigas rose, and Zaphreth remembered to get to his feet and bow as the king left.

CHAPTER 26

Zaphreth stood outside the door of lea-wood that led to the King's private chambers. The weight of the door troubled him, ancient wood that had seen centuries of weather and time, and then been hewed and planed and carved with a relief of the rising Day-Star and all that drew its life from it: trees and birds and horses and men, and in the top corner of the main panel of the door, the outline of a dragon in flight.

Zaphreth had not known what to expect, whether the King would summon him to a court, or simply have him thrown in the dungeon. But the personal summons had come that morning during breakfast. Zaphreth had followed the server through the palace, wondering if he should just make a run for it. But something about the server's peaceful pacing told him that he would make things much worse if he tried anything stupid.

Chewing on his lip, Zaphreth raised his fist to tap on the door, but could not quite bring himself to do it. His mind kept turning on the unbodying of Lur, the blaze of light and the charred circle. What if that was to be his end? What if the Lord of Callenlas saw fit to unbody him, Zaphreth, for selling Callenlas into Lur's hand?

"Enter."

The summons was light and inviting, but Zaphreth jumped (he had not knocked, after all), and swallowed hard before pushing the door open. He bowed low and waited to be greeted before rising.

"Zaphreth," the King spoke with a smile, and when Zaphreth straightened, he found him resting on a padded couch, propped up by feather cushions and covered in a blanket woven of undyed sheep's wool. The image was in such contrast with the warrior Zaphreth had encountered previously that he found it hard at first to reconcile the two men. Yet when he dared, finally, to look into the King's face he found there that same serious smile, that same welcoming yet piercing gaze, and the sense of restful power that had been present on the platform outside the city.

"Are you recovering, Sir?" Zaphreth asked, in a small voice.

"I am, thanks in no small part to the ministrations of my many attendants." Amusement flickered in the corners of the King's mouth. He glanced around at the vases of flowers which cluttered every available surface, along with jugs of water, bowls of fruit, and even a tray of marzipan mice.

"Come and sit by me, Zaphreth," the King gestured to a padded footstool, and Zaphreth sat gingerly on its edge.

"How are you finding the palace?" the King asked.

Zaphreth nodded and mumbled incoherently. He seemed to be finding it difficult to get words in order and onto his tongue. He drew a deep breath. "I am very grateful to you for my room and food."

The polite conversation was now unbearable.

"Please, Sir," Zaphreth blurted, "What will you do to me?"

The King looked with pity on Zaphreth, but with his eyes to the ground Zaphreth could not see his expression.

"I know," said the King gently.

"You know?" Zaphreth's head jerked up in surprise.

"I knew you were a servant of Lur when you came to the camp. I know that you told Lur to attack."

Zaphreth's mind whirled.

"Why didn't you stop me?"

"I hoped you would choose differently."

Zaphreth felt himself curling over as his final, desperate grasp at self-defence was removed.

"What will you do to me?" Zaphreth asked miserably.

"What will I do?"

"I am a traitor. I betrayed you. I betrayed your people."

"You acted as you were – a servant of Lur. You had made me no oath. You were deceitful, but you had no promise to break. Do not take up more burden than is yours to carry, Zaphreth."

Zaphreth's face writhed with the effort of understanding. The coils of guilt that had bound him for the past week unfurled slightly, with a prickling relief that he might not, at least, suffer the same fate as Lur.

"You are still unhappy?" the King asked, leaning in slightly.

"I'm afraid," Zaphreth said in a choked voice, still with his eyes closed. "I've been a bit of a fool."

As he said it, he realised that Elior was perhaps the only person he could voice this fear to. Perhaps Runa, said a small voice in his mind, but no, Zaphreth shook his head vigorously. Runa would agree, scornfully perhaps. No doubt she would want no more to do with him now.

"I thought I was a prince, you see," Zaphreth confessed, still with his eyes closed. "I thought I should be treated better because of it; I thought I should be honoured. I have watched you ... you are not like that; no one is like that here. It was such a relief to not be a nobody anymore."

Daring to open his eyes, Zaphreth found Elior's eyes creased with amusement, but not the unkind sort. It felt as though Elior was sharing Zaphreth's shame and smiling with him.

"A bit of a fool," Elior agreed. "But at least you know you have been a fool. There are far too many who live their whole lives in foolishness while thinking themselves very wise. That is far more unfortunate. You have a great opportunity to step out of foolishness into wisdom."

Zaphreth drew an uneven breath.

"That's not the worst of it, though," he said, wishing he could shut his eyes again. He plucked at the ends of his belt, twisting the lengths into each other as he worked up the courage to unburden himself.

"I have been worse than a fool," he said at last. "I was cruel ... to my mother."

Elior now appeared very grave, and pain flooded his eyes.

"This is worse," Elior confirmed, and Zaphreth cringed. Perhaps now Elior would see him as he really was. "But in my experience, a mother's love is not easily lost."

"But that's not what I mean,"

"What troubles you really, Zaphreth?"

"I used to think that evil and bad things were outside, out there, waiting to harm me or make me bad."

The King waited in listening silence while Zaphreth

fought to express feelings and thoughts he had not even articulated to himself before.

"But I was bad. I chose evil," Zaphreth raised a miserable face to the King. "I was cruel to my mother; I lied to Runa, to *you* ... I deceived you all. I should have refused to Send to Lur, or at least just not Sent anything. But I was a coward. And I knew ... I knew all along that it wasn't right. I couldn't think why at the time; all my training, everything I had been taught told me I was doing right, but inside I knew. Deep down. The bad was *in me.*

"And I don't know what to do about that," Zaphreth continued, his misery growing. "Evil *out there* ... I can fight that. I can use a sword; I can use my mind. I'd even fight Lur himself if it came down to it, though I know I should lose. But the evil in me, in *here* ..." Zaphreth pressed a hand against his chest, where the core of him ached like an ember. "It's too big. However much I want to do right, however much I want to be good and whole and true like you ... I can't."

Zaphreth's shoulders rounded over his hunched core, which felt as vast and dry and dead as the Southern Desert. The King sighed heavily, and Zaphreth's heart sank further. The admission had cost him everything: his pride, his self-esteem. He knew he could not have told anyone else, not even Runa. He fully expected the King to gravely send him back to tSardia. How could he remain, with so much weakness and darkness pulsing inside him?

The King flicked his blanket aside, lifting his legs off his footstool with a grunt of effort. He sat forward, forearms on his knees in a posture of earnestness.

"Zaphreth," he said, his voice every bit as grave as Zaphreth had anticipated. "Zaphreth, in all my years on this earth – and there have been many – I have met only a small number who were as honest and truthful with themselves as you. All my advisors, all the princes, queens and kings I have encountered, and all the hardworking men and women under them too – they all cling to something good in themselves. They try as hard as they can to run and hide from the obvious truth, that no matter how great the evil outside, the real danger comes from within.

"It is human prejudice, human greed, human selfishness, anger, desire, pride ... these are the things that damage the world. Lur simply capitalised on the human capacity for evil. It is a sad, but undeniable truth that the human heart is warped, bent so that it tends to evil, not in every instance, but more often than the good. It is, perhaps, the hardest thing to admit.

"Do you know how rare you are, Zaphreth?"

Zaphreth shook his head, and finally dared to lift his eyes to the King's. His wise and kind eyes looked back, meeting Zaphreth's, welcoming his gaze.

"What can I do?" Zaphreth asked, for as much as the King's response gave him hope, he had provided no solution.

"I have already done everything necessary," King Elior replied. "You had bound yourself to Lur in blood; I have paid the redemption price. You are now mine."

Zaphreth's heart pounded, and he knelt impulsively at the King's feet. He took King Elior's hand in his and kissed it.

"My King," he said. "I will serve you in any way I can. My life is yours to command."

"Thank you, dear son," King Elior clasped Zaphreth's hand. "But what I wish is for you to be free. Free to do those things you desire – to be wise, and kind, and generous, forgiving, loving, honest, loyal, brave."

"I cannot ..." Zaphreth whispered.

"Stand."

Zaphreth rose to his feet, and the King pressed his palm, warm and heavy, against Zaphreth's chest, on the very place that ached with longing and unmet desire. Zaphreth felt a sensation, like coolness and warmth together, spreading from his chest through blood and bone, until he felt his entire being consumed with light.

"I give you life, Zaphreth son of Irek. The life of a star."

The King removed his hand and the sensation diminished slowly, but without leaving Zaphreth feeling emptied in any way. Instead, he felt whole, complete, for the first time in his life.

"Now, this is no magic," the King said, with a note of caution. "No trick to make you suddenly good. You must still choose. Some choices may be harder than others. But you now have the eternal light of the stars in your soul. You will find you love the things I love, and the more you choose them, the easier it will become.

"But I must give you one more warning. A soul imbued with the life of a star is eternal. If you begin to choose evil again, deliberately, consistently, you will become as twisted and as dark as Lur himself, until your light goes out. And then there is no redemption."

Zaphreth nodded, still overwhelmed.

"And now I had better put my blanket back on, before my healers return and banish me back to bed," the King said with a twinkle in his eye. He sank back against the pillows with a sigh that made Zaphreth think perhaps he was not as near being healed as he had said.

Zaphreth sat back down on the footstool again, still feeling as though the world had been unmade and then restored again. There was a new quality to the light, and Zaphreth found himself breathing as though the very air was fragile, and he might break the moment. He did not want to leave.

"I have something to ask you, Zaphreth," the King said,

after a long pause.

"Yes, my Lord," Zaphreth replied, "Anything."

The King smiled warmly.

"Remember that you are free," he said gently. "There will be times when I command you, but this is not one of those times. You are free to agree or to deny me this request. You may wish simply to live a quiet life with your parents, and that is a wonderful thing.

"You know that I have journeyed through many lands during my years on this earth. Callenlas was the first place I came, and the first place to submit to my leading. However, there are other realms who are in desperate need of my guidance and authority. Some have already begun to live by the ways of the stars, but others need persuading still. I am in need of people who will serve me, who will lead these nations as the first princes of Callenlas led this people. I look for men and women like you, who know their weaknesses, who long to do right."

"I do not think I am the right person, Sir," Zaphreth replied slowly. "I have not been trained as a prince or a leader. I was just a poor apprentice before I joined the army."

"Training counts far less than character," the King replied. "Though I would provide a few years of teaching with my Masters, especially to hone your mind's strength, and teach you my law and history.

"Most would hold out to you the honour and prestige of being the ruler of a nation, however small. Most would offer you wealth and titles to entice you. I offer none of that. To be a good ruler means to deny oneself, to give up all rights to one's own freedom and happiness. A good ruler lives for the good of his people, not himself. A good ruler is the first in any battle charge and the last to leave; in times of famine, he must go without to feed the hungry; in times of plenty he must use the resources available to care for the poor and those who cannot adequately provide for themselves. You must hold back those who would seek to use power for their own ends and uphold laws that may be unpopular but are for good.

"But Zaphreth, you could do great good. You could be a source of great joy and happiness to an entire nation, and that would bring me great joy.

"Think it over, and tell me your decision, after you have been reunited with your mother. There is no great rush. And now, perhaps you will step out onto the terrace for a moment. There is someone loitering outside my door ..."

CHAPTER 27

The loitering someone was Runa. A server had summoned her, but she could hear the King's voice within the room and did not want to interrupt.

"Come inside, dear daughter," the King called suddenly.

Sheepishly, Runa pushed open the door and crept in. King Elior smiled, his welcome making her wonder why she had hesitated to enter.

"Come and sit with me," he gestured to a padded stool near his seat. Runa took it gladly.

"Are you feeling better?" she asked, shyly.

"Much better," he answered with a smile. "Thank you for the mice."

Runa's face brightened.

"Everyone sends fruit when someone's ill," she said, wrinkling her nose in bafflement. "But sweets are much better."

291

"I quite agree," the King said solemnly. "Would you like one?"

Runa went to fetch the plate, and they sat together, enjoying the sticky sweetness in silence.

"You have been quite the heroine," the King said, once his mouse had disappeared.

"I wouldn't say that," Runa ducked her head.

"Nor should you," the King laughed softly. "But I may say it, and I do. You were braver than many of my trained riders, and more determined."

"Thank you," Runa whispered. Her mind turned over her recent adventures, and though the memory of hunger and sleeping on a forest floor was vivid and far from comfortable, something in her ached at the thought of going back to Feldemoore, back to lessons and dresses and the panelled walls of the library.

"I don't think I was meant to be a princess," Runa sighed glumly, dropping her chin into her hand. "I seem to want all the wrong things."

The King smiled fondly at her bended head.

"Perhaps it would help you to know that the stars find their places in the Fields of Light by no accident, but are placed carefully, by a loving hand. And no less is true of those who look to them for light."

Runa glanced doubtfully at the King.

"Perhaps there is some great service that only you

may render your people and this island. Perhaps you have been born a princess for a very good reason."

Runa sat straighter.

"I think it makes me a better princess," she said, "to have a knowledge of war and dragons. I could give good advice on a council."

"Certainly," King Elior agreed. "But I have been speaking with your father. He tells me that the dragon fleet of Feldemoore is lagging behind Callenlas in the quality of training. He wishes to begin an exchange programme, where young sky riders in training could come to Orr and share our dragon lore. And we would send our novice riders to Feldemoore, to learn mountain tracking and hunting."

"That's nice," Runa said politely.

"I wondered if you would wish to join the students?"

Runa swallowed hard. Her heart was suddenly beating very fast and loud. She could barely speak.

"I would love to, my King, but I have duties. My father wants me to study at Lelanta."

"I think you might find your father more willing to let you go, now he has seen what you are capable of."

Runa wanted to cry. She wanted to run and jump about like the hoyden she was trying hard not to be anymore.

What she did instead was kneel and kiss the King's hand. Her eyes were overbright, and she was using so much energy to keep her body still that she could not speak.

The King allowed Runa to process his news for some moments in silence.

"My dear," he said at last. "There is one request I make of you, before you can be admitted to the training for sky riders."

"Anything," Runa said, brightly.

"One of the vows of new riders is that they will forgive injury, rather than seeking vengeance. And if they have a serious claim to wrong, they will bring it to a senior rider, or to me. I want you to demonstrate that you are willing to keep this vow."

Runa frowned, suspicious.

"Zaphreth," the King said.

Runa's shoulders slumped and her face closed.

"I can't ..." she whispered. "You don't understand."

"Don't I?"

Runa looked up into Elior's kind eyes and saw traces of pain. Of course, in all his years among human beings, he had known betrayal again and again. How many friends had turned against him?

But the taste of Zaphreth's deceit was still bitter in her mouth.

"I don't know how," she said.

"You must tell him what he did to you," the King said.

"And see what he says. He was bound by a blood oath, and wrongly taught. You cannot be angry with him for that. And perhaps," King Elior added, in his gentlest tone yet. "Perhaps you should have been a little more discerning, in simply accepting the word of a tSardian."

Runa bit back her rejection of such a suggestion, remembering just in time who she was talking to. She swallowed hard.

"Perhaps," she managed to concede.

"Zaphreth is on the terrace," the King said.

Runa pulled a face.

ઈ ✳ ର

The terrace looked out over the west of the city, and now stood in the full heat of the Day-Star. Stone benches were set against the wall of the palace, and a stone rail ran around its edge, to prevent anyone falling into the garden below. Several large pots, painted colourfully and studded with tiny mirrors, held tall plants with large, waving leaves, which provided some shade. The mirrors threw tiny rainbow reflections onto the tiles.

Zaphreth sat on a bench after he left King Elior, and simply waited. He felt too full even to think; and a peace that he had never imagined throbbed in his limbs and chest. It was almost unbearable, like the sweetness of honey.

Sounds of the palace drifted up to him, but only added to his feeling of rest; the clatter of pans, the sweep of bristles against stone, the low chatter of two female servers from a window below.

Then the curtains to the room billowed out slightly, and Runa stepped onto the terrace with him.

Zaphreth stood at once. The awkwardness returned but did not overwhelm him. He wanted Runa's friendship, but not so desperately as before. He felt that even without it, he would be all right.

"You were my friend," Runa said, her face twisted in a look of pain.

"I'm sorry," Zaphreth said.

"No, you don't understand," Runa sighed heavily, her green eyes brimming with tears. This seemed to make her angry, and she wiped her nose roughly with the back of her hand. "You don't understand how lonely it is. You were my first friend. The first person who ever saw me as I really am."

Zaphreth looked at her, this fireball of a girl who had saved his life and two kingdoms in one week. She was no beauty, but her vivid passion was keenly attractive. The hurt in her eyes was painful to see.

"Runa, I'm sorry," Zaphreth said earnestly. "I didn't understand what I was doing, but that's no excuse. I shouldn't have lied to you. I wish I hadn't."

Runa sniffed aggressively and turned to look out over the city, her hands resting in curled fists on the stone rail.

"What did the King say?" she asked.

"He forgave me," Zaphreth answered with wonder. He found he could not express with words everything that had occurred in the King's presence. "He asked me to travel with him, to help him in other lands."

Runa nodded, a little dismally.

"So, you'll be going away, then."

"Not at first," Zaphreth said. "I mean, I haven't decided yet but …"

"It's hard to say no to him," Runa finished the sentence for him. Their eyes met with shared understanding, and suddenly everything was all right again.

"I am sorry," Zaphreth said again. "Friends?"

Runa nodded, and he felt brave enough to draw near her. Together they looked out over the roofs of Orr to the plains beyond.

EPILOGUE

The rider travelled at a comfortable trot along the King's Highway, his horse stepping happily over the beaten earth. Sitting straight in the saddle, the traveller seemed distracted, allowing the horse to pick its way along the road, which it did without trouble – this was a route it knew well.

At length, the horse turned off the main highway onto a well-kept track that led through some fruit trees, providing a welcome shade from the full summer heat of the Day-Star. The track wound on for about half a mile, beneath clusters of ripening apples and pears, before branching into two. The left way ran through a broad vineyard, still in the early days of development, but already looking healthy and well-tended. The horse took the track to the right and drew to a halt outside a pleasant little house with newly whitewashed walls, and a thatch roof. A clean stable stood to the side of the house, and some chickens scratched in the dirt around the door.

"Zaphreth!" the woman who emerged from the house was small, her greying hair pulled into a neat bun. She dried her hands on her apron as she hurried forward, wrapping her arms tightly around the young man who had just dismounted. The warm welcome seemed to startle him out of his deep thoughts, and he returned the hug warmly, kissing his mother on her round, rosy cheek.

"I'm so glad you came," Ama smiled eagerly, a slight twinkle in her eyes as she took the horse's bridle and led it into the stable.

Irek ducked under the lintel of the stable to step out and put his broad arm around Zaphreth's shoulder.

"You got away, then!" he said in his expansive voice, ruffling Zaphreth's hair as if he was still a boy of fourteen, instead of a grown man employed in King Elior's service.

"The King was most insistent, once he knew you'd asked me to come," Zaphreth said. "He practically pushed me out of the door."

"He keeps you busy enough," Irek said, without a trace of resentment. "You've earned a couple of days off. And we have a surprise ..."

"Hush!" Ama called from the stable, where she was removing the horse's tack, and setting out fresh hay and water.

"Sorry!" Irek touched his finger to his lip and gave Zaphreth a wink. "Come and try some wine – I've just opened a cask from the harvest two years ago, and it's quite good. Not good enough for the King yet, but we're getting there."

Zaphreth followed his father into the house with a grin. Already he could feel the burden of his duties slipping from his shoulders, though it usually took him a while to fully relax when he left Orr. Irek spoke truth when he said the King kept Zaphreth busy. Since his training was completed at the age of eighteen, Zaphreth had first spent a few years with the King's Masters, studying the gift, and learning to put his Mind Powers to best use. He had then spent two years working for the Ambassador of tSardia, which had meant long, frequent visits to tSama on the far south coast, and boring but difficult negotiations, when he had tried to persuade the tSardians to enact the terms of a peace treaty with Callenlas. Now he had a new commission, but he was not sure how to break the news to his parents.

"Here, try this," Irek placed a pewter goblet on the table in front of him, half-full of a rich, red wine. Zaphreth obediently took a sip.

"Hm, it's good," he said, with surprise. His father had imported vines from tSardia, sending for the best ones from the east, and was working towards producing the wine he had once made for King Lakesh. Vines took a long time to mature, however, and Zaphreth had been expecting his father to take several more years to reach wine of this quality.

"I could take some for the King when I return," Zaphreth offered.

"Not yet, not yet," Irek shook his head. "It's better than I expected, but it will take a few more years to reach the quality I want. This will do for the local trade."

Ama bustled in and began to set the table with enough food to feast ten.

"I'll never eat all this," Zaphreth sighed, knowing his mother would expect him to eat double what he needed. He should have thought to wear looser trousers.

Ama laughed, that twinkle still in her eye.

"Have you heard from Runa?" she asked, putting a plate heaped with scones on the boards in front of Zaphreth.

"Not recently," Zaphreth said. "She was posted to Meretheos, and her letters ... let's say she still finds writing a chore."

Irek laughed.

"She's a firebrand, that girl," he said approvingly, and Zaphreth smiled with his father. His parents had embraced Runa fully and had often invited her to stay while she was completing her training in Orr. She had delighted in their simple life, and once Ama and Irek realised that she actually wanted to shrug off the trappings of royalty, they let her help clean out the goats, and Ama even taught Runa how to cook. Well, she tried. The oatcakes Runa produced under Ama's supervision were charred and determinedly not round, but Irek ate them with relish, and Ama pronounced them 'excellent'. It was annoying, Zaphreth felt, especially when they expected such high standards from him, but he found it hard to begrudge Runa anything.

"Do you have a new commission from the King?" Irek asked, reaching out a hand to take a scone. Ama smacked his hand away gently, even as she placed a bowl of spiced stewed apple next to the scones.

"Wait," she said firmly, and Irek grumbled but waited.

"Well," Zaphreth drew a breath. He had wanted to discuss this later in the evening, but now that his father had asked, he had no choice. "Actually, yes. King Elior is planning to travel soon, to return to the lands oversees where others follow his laws. There are many nations at war who need his peace."

Ama had become very still, and Zaphreth knew she already apprehended what he was about to say.

"King Elior wondered if I would go with him. He has an outpost in a place called Bhari-Ta, and he wants me to manage it for a while."

"How far away?"

"It will take us a month to travel over sea and land," Zaphreth replied slowly.

Ama silently took a jug and took it outside to the well.

"You should go," Irek said quickly and quietly, while Ama was outside. "Don't let us keep you here, Zaphreth. You must live your life. We have the vines, and the goats. And Runa."

Zaphreth smiled softly and nodded his thanks to his father.

Ama came in and set the jug on the table. Slowly she put her arms around Zaphreth's shoulders and kissed his hair.

"You will have wonderful adventures," she said softly, a smile on her lips and tears in her eyes. "But you must write often. Not like Runa."

"I will write with every delegation that returns," he said. "And I can Send often. We've been working on using crystals to augment Sendings – Master Terras has discovered that creodil has the best effect, especially when ..."

Zaphreth noticed the slight glaze in his parents' eyes. They always listened politely to his work, but he knew it did not really interest them. To his mind, this progress with crystals was thrilling, and could change the world, opening the possibility of communication between lands far apart. His parents' world, however, was wide enough for them, with the vineyard and the local town. Even their occasional trips to Orr to visit him had overwhelmed them, though Irek had eyed the capital's beautiful buildings with admiration and enjoyed the bustle of the markets there.

"I will Send," he concluded softly, squeezing Ama's arm.

The trees outside began to rustle as if a storm was blowing up. Ama and Irek exchanged an excited glance.

"Come," Irek said to Zaphreth, and the three of them stepped out into the yard.

Overhead soared a beautiful mountain blue, wings flapping as it circled in to land, its belly a silver blush against its vivid azure scales. Zaphreth and his parents shielded their eyes as the dragon banked steeply and came gracefully to land, stopping just in front of the house. Its purple eyes gleamed and its long tail coiled as the great wings fluttered and folded against its sides.

"Well done, Shari-girl," the sky rider called out merrily, unbuckling her hood and patting the long neck affectionately. "Perfect landing."

Zaphreth felt a glow of pleasure as the rider swung her leg over the shoulders of the dragon and waved enthusiastically at the welcome party by the house.

"Two days from Ildos to Orr," she whooped. "I reckon that's a record!"

With a grin of greeting, Runa alighted.

ABOUT THE AUTHOR

H. R. Hess is married to Steffan, and mum to three children. Having enjoyed many adventures from her armchair (and many a bus-stop, waiting room, and home-made den) she decided to write her own.

Also by Ref Light

Extracted
Rich Castro

Fifteen-year-old Trey has just moved to England from
America. Struggling to fit in with his new life, everything
changes when he is extracted to Anasius, an alternate
world on the brink of war.

Available to buy from ReformationLightning.com

Read More Ref Light

Reformation Lightning specialise in creative Christian
writing for young readers.

To find out more and to buy our books visit:
ReformationLightning.com